HOLDING OUT FOR FOREVER

BlackPath MC Book Three

VERA QUINN

COPYRIGHT

Printed in the United States

Cover: Tracey Douglas@ Dark Water Covers

Editor & Formatter: Maggie Kern

ISBN: 9781534684607

******WARNING******

This book is intended for adults 18+ only. Violence, strong language, and sexual situations. If any of this offends you, please, this book is not for you.
*******WARNING*******

This series is continuing. This will be a series of four books and some novellas.

ACKNOWLEDGMENTS

I'd like to say thank you to family and friends. Charles, you are my better half and my rock always.

Again, and I can never say this enough, Liberty, Cree, and Johnna you are my support every day. During the writing of this book I brought on my new PA Johnna Seibert and this lady can do anything and in no time.

Kori, Nicole, and Shanna, thank you for pimping my books. You ladies are the best. Executives in charge of pimping and doing it supremely. That is the title I went with, but any way you look at it, they are great.

Tracey and Julie, you two are priceless. I thank my lucky stars the day we were put in contact.

Everyone in my author group who I interact with, it has been a joy to get to know you. Everyone that is on my author page, thank you for liking and checking in. This is the first place you will find all things Author Vera Quinn.
Every single author, PA, and blogger who has reached out to me

and welcomed me. I thank you. To all the groups that share my stuff. Thank you for all the shares and comments.

I'm not a real social person. My husband, Charles, says I am the most anti-social person he knows. I'm not anti-social, I just don't talk something to death, and I like to get to the punchline fast. I don't have a very good sense of humor. I like to look someone in the eye when I talk to them. So, this is work for me to be social, but I try. Charles is the life of the party, so opposites do attract. I freeze up in crowds, so he anchors me. But I cherish every interaction I have with you. So, don't give up on me.

To everyone that bought or read my books, thank you.
Now this is my place to speak, so here is what I have to say. Thank you for the reviews I have gotten. I appreciate everyone. Good and bad. I try to learn something out of every single one. I know it sounds like the same standard comment from an author, but it isn't. I like to hear your likes and dislikes. If the book is too long or too short. How it flows. If I forget something or I go overboard with something. I try to keep my stories fresh and my storyline unpredictable. My characters are who they are, and they expand as the storyline is developing. I don't promise HEA for everyone. I don't promise I won't have cliffhangers, but I will state it clearly from now on when it has one. I won't promise a character you like won't die in my story. I won't promise that no one ever gets cheated on. All I say is I will try to give you a great read. I'm not going by anyone else's formula, only mine. If this is what you can accept, then sit back and get comfortable, because I am going to do my best to make you laugh, make you cry, make you yell, make you want to see someone get run over by a bull-dozer, and just make you want more, even though the story is complete or until next time. So, I'll quit talking it to death and just try to do it....

CAST OF CHARACTERS

BlackPath MC

Officers:

Cameron "Chief" Black- President

Trent "Driller" Black- Vice- President -wife- Laurie

ZMan- SAA - Ol' Lady-Kelsey

Hambone- Road Captain -Ol' lady Kelsey

Hammer- Treasurer Blake "Trigger" Trammel-Enforcer

Cutter- Secretary

Brain- Intel/Tech guy

Patched Members:

Ty "Tazer" Black

Jeb "Shield" Jameson

Woody "Killman"

Sinner

Demon

Prospect: Todd

Club Girls: Joy, Lita, Sas, and Fawn

Feral Steel MC:

Steel- President - Ol' Lady & Wife- Kat Daughter- Kim

Kylar "Devil" Steel- Vice-President Wife - Callie

Hacksaw- SAA

Buzz-Road Captain

Keifer "Stone" Steel- Treasurer

Tito- Intel man

Leads - Tech Man

Ax- Secretary

Patched Members:

Fugulist

Pick

Tugman

Bower

Troubled Fathoms MC:

Hawser - President Mother in-law- Betsy Clark

Miner - Vice President

Andrew "Dra" Stevens- SAA

Krill (River) – Enforcer

Club Girls - Lottie

Rebellions 4 Blood MC:

DeWayne "Diamondback" Mahan - President

Mason "Sarge" Brumley

Cru London "Stealth" Jameson

Aaron "Braun" Mahn

NOTE FROM AUTHOR

PROLOGUE

HOLDING OUT FOR *FOREVER*

BLACKPATH MC BOOK THREE

C hief...

You can never go back. This is so true. No matter how much you want to. If so, I would have never left my friend alone when he needed me. I would have paid better attention to what was going on. Tried to control it and headed it off. Tommy would still be alive.

I would have never trusted Cheryl. Can't say I wouldn't have still hooked up with her or I wouldn't have Ty, but I damn sure would have cut her loose sooner and protected my heart better, and never given her my trust.

I would have told Grandma Sue I loved and appreciated her more. That lady was my rock and I never appreciated her enough.

I would have respected Whiskey more. Better known as Dad, but I think I respected him more as a brother. My president in the BlackPath MC.

I would have protected Callie more from Devil. Callie was only eighteen and I should have made the decision, but I thought

1

since Tommy was her brother, she should have the choice, I regret that now. I could have protected her from the pain life gave her.

I should have sent Kim packing the first night she approached me. I shouldn't have taken her up on her little get-even-with-dad plan, but then again, I wouldn't have what I have now.

Regrets, regrets, and more regrets, but life moves on. I keep learning. Now I have the woman I love, and I wouldn't change that for anything. We have expanded our family and life is good, but don't think you can guess what life has given me, because no one knows what fate holds...not even me.

CHAPTER ONE

HOLDING OUT FOR *FOREVER*

BLACKPATH MC BOOK THREE

C hief...

I'm going out of my head with worry trying to make things right for Callie. That girl has taken off, but she had good reason. Devil, Steel, Karen, and I, all gave her reasons to take off. She learned her lessons too well growing up. I taught her to be independent, strong, and resourceful, and she is that. Now she's in Colorado, and I don't think she'll be coming home anytime soon.

When we were there, she ended up getting herself shot. That Dra seems the protective type, and he has a good club to back him up. Now it's time to tie up all the loose ends. We were reacting to things before, but since then I've had time to do some thinking, we have things to take care of.

I'm sitting at the bar in the clubhouse waiting for Tazer, Driller, and ZMan. We have some thinking to do, out loud. Things have been messy, and where there's a mess, someone fucked up. We'll get our answers. I hear the bikes pull up out front. It's so quiet here. No music, parties, or crowds. Just what we need to figure this out and where we need to go from here.

3

I reach for a bottle of Jack and some glasses. I notice Jeb is with the brothers as they walk in. We haven't voted him in, but it's just a formality we haven't taken care of, yet. He took a bullet for me, even if it wasn't serious, and that will get him his patch. I already have his road name picked out. It'll be his soon. I'll get Kelsey to get on his cut. I take my phone out and shoot her a text while everyone makes it over to the bar.

"We have some loose ends to tie up and we have to come up with a plan to handle the Feral Steel MC and Diamondback. Where are we?" I look to each of them. "Jeb you can stay. No one outside these walls hears what's said. In fact, let's go to my office." I pick up the bottle of Jack. Tazer and Jeb pick up the glasses, and we head to the office.

"We have a lead on who shot at Callie outside the bar the night of her graduation. Feral's tech guy Tito has family here, and one of the girls who works at his family's café says Stone is unhappy with some shit going on. In fact, they have a lot of unrest in their family. The mom, Kat, is not happy with Steel or Devil. The daughter, Kim, is acting out. Remember, she's the reason Callie got sent to the hospital when she was in Oklahoma. Stone isn't happy with anything going on in the club or family. Word is he orchestrated it. If we can get the information—Steel and Devil should be able to get it—but they have their heads up their asses and aren't taking care of business." Tazer has uncovered valuable information. I understand Steel and Devil's minds have been in other places, so have ours, but I need to find out how far this goes and what the blowback will be for us, and Callie.

"What is Stone's beef with Callie? He's Devil's brother, if that isn't some shit. Got any hard evidence? Was the target Callie or Devil?" No one, especially a Steel, has a right to be hating on Callie. I need answers. "I know all about Kim acting out. She's been showing up around my house, and everyone knows she even came by here when we were in Colorado. We've been talk-ing. Keeping my options open with her." All my brothers are giving me the look. They want me to give up information, but for now I'll play it close to the vest.

"We also know for sure Diamondback has more children. He has a son, Aaron, road name used to be Braun. No one has seen him in a while. Heard there was an argument when Diamondback put his plan in motion about Callie. Diamondback wanted heirs, well word is Braun can't have children. He felt slighted and took off." I had heard that, but Diamondback is acting like Callie is his only child. *Wait, Tazer said children.*

"How many children, and why wouldn't he tell Callie if she had more siblings?" There's nothing that man does that doesn't have a reason.

"He also has twin daughters here in Texas somewhere. We are digging. Seems like Diamondback thinks his days are going to be coming to an end sooner rather than later, and he made a will. A will Brain has tracked down and managed to get a copy of. Him and Hambone are on their way back now, they will have the answers." ZMan fills our glasses as he tells me about the will.

"So, we have unrest in the Steel family, and Diamondback is being his usual devious self. Did anyone find anything out about why Blake decided to show his face again?" This is the other wildcard I don't like. He left this family two years ago to go deep undercover. He had been trying to dig things up on Rye and Bourbon when he left. I told him not to show his face around here again without an apology. My uncles would not have had anything to do with Whiskey's death. End of story. But Blake thought he should dig, and he came up with jack shit.

"From what we've found, everything he's said has checked out. Callie called him for help. He had finished his last undercover assignment and was on an extended vacation. He's transferred to

Colorado, but there is something going on with one of his superiors. They have a real hate for each other. He wanted Blake back undercover, this time it was in a motorcycle club, but Blake refused. He said he didn't investigate clubs undercover anymore. The superior wants his badge." Jeb has been on Blake, and the information he just gave is helpful. Blake didn't go back on his promise to stay away from any club investigations. At least he's not a liar.

"Would we let Trigger come back if he wanted? He may be walking away from his job. He was BlackPath MC. We voted to let him walk away." ZMan and Blake were good friends just like he and I were. Trigger, I haven't heard that name in a long time.

"A vote took him out and it would take another vote to bring him back. Not until he apologizes in front of the club and he hangs up that badge for good. Even then, could we really trust him?" Walking away was never taken lightly

"What do you mean, you're keeping your options open with Kim, and are we still not letting Callie know that the fallout you and Blake had was not about that bitch Tina?" Driller has a point, maybe we should let Callie know the truth. No, that's club business, and I try to keep her out of it.

"It means that Kim is coming over tonight, and I'm going to see just how far she wants to go to piss Steel off. Callie doesn't need to know anything about mine and Blake's problems. Just let her assume what she wants. That way no one is lying. I'll deal with Kimberly Steel. I have a bad feeling about the situation with Dra's club. When Brain wraps up the thing with Diamondback, I want him to do some digging." ZMan and Driller both look at me like I need my head examined. "I have to know the situation Callie is in is safe. The last time I talked to her, she said Dra is keeping more than one prospect on her and Betsy. That's not normal. I have a bad feeling about it, and I won't let my daughter get dragged into their shit. Even if she is Dra's ol' lady, she'll always be my daughter."

"I agree." Ty is the first to agree.

"Me, too. Something seemed off when I talked to her two days ago." Jeb doesn't usually say anything about what he talks to Callie about, so I know it's not just me being overprotective.

"If it's their club business, they're not going to like us poking around." ZMan is always the voice of reason until he loses that cool temper.

"I don't give a fuck what they like. Callie has been shot twice in the last year, and I don't want it to be three times." Everyone knows better than to argue when it comes to family safety.

"Point taken. I'll be sure he gets on it." ZMan knows I'm serious, so he'll get it taken care of.

"Callie will be here in two weeks for her doctor visit, so anyone that talks to her, pay close attention to what she says about her life in Colorado. She's not going to say anything on her own. She'd look at that as a betrayal of Dra. If she is safe, I don't care about the Troubled Fathom's activities. Let's just not miss anything." It was so much easier when I had Callie here. Now, as her dad, I just worry constantly. Shaking my head, I go back to club business.

"Jeb, have you heard from Sarge and Stealth?" Jeb goes stiff. I know he's in a tough situation. Sarge has been his best friend for years, and Stealth his twin brother. "Look, I'm not asking for you to spy on your blood, or your friend, for the club. I just want to make sure Sarge causes no problems. We all know he's the one that took Karen out, with those other two bitches. Taking out women goes against who he used to be. I just want to make sure he's not going to go off the deep end and go after anyone else."

7

Jeb knows I'm talking about Callie, but if Sarge is affected, he could go off on anyone.

"Sarge is just different. He's quiet and distant. Stealth and I are both worried about him, but he'll work it out." Jeb looks uncomfortable talking about it. I still need to keep an eye on Sarge.

"We having any problems with any of our businesses? We need to have church tomorrow night six sharp. No one is late. We vote on Jeb getting his cut and all business matters at hand. We are going to have to get one of the ol' ladies to get the club girls in line or give the job to Joy. She's the oldest girl and has been here the longest. She knows her place and keeps the others in line as best she can. If we go with Joy, she gets a paycheck with benefits. It's a full-time job. She's been here ten years, so she has earned it, but it has to go for a vote." I've been keeping close tabs on the club, even if my mind has been in other places. I never neglect the club.

"Chief, you may have your hands full with Sas. She thinks she has some claim on you. I heard her and Lita going at it last night. Sas got wind of Lita giving you a blowjob at lunch yesterday, and she was pissed. I threw her ass out last night." Jeb should have called me, but I know now.

"Jeb, if there is any more trouble with Sas, you give me a call. No woman owns my cock, and I fuck who I want. She'll be finding her ass barred from the clubhouse." I've fucked that woman a couple of times, and she gave me head a few times. She was nothing special. Another faceless pussy is all she is to me. Since Cheryl, that's all they have ever been. It's been a lot of years. When one starts trying to get too close, I chase their asses off. Relationships are too complicated, and I don't need that in my life. "Anything else we need to go over? Any other problems? When will Brain and Hambone be back?"

"In the morning," ZMan puts in.

"Okay. I will be here by noon to be brought up to date. We have church tomorrow night. Let everyone know everything but do it quietly. I want Braun found, too. I'd like a sit-down with him. Was he an officer in the club or do we know?" More and more questions keep popping into my head. I don't like loose ends, or not knowing what's up.

"Maybe Brain knows." Driller could be right.

"Tonight, I play a cat-and-mouse game with a pussy, but by the time I'm done I will have some answers." I look at my watch and I know I have to get moving. "Unless it is life or death, do not disturb me tonight. Tazer, stay here at the club. I want as many answers as I can get out of Kim."

"Doesn't hurt she's smoking hot. Be sure to let your brain and not your cock lead you. What if she was sent?" I have thought of that, but she has given me no reason not to trust her, yet, but ZMan has a good point.

"My eyes are wide open." I have to see where this goes. She may have the answer as to why Stone would have something against Callie. "Only one woman has ever gotten over on me, and it won't happen again, ever. Later." With that I get up and leave. I know they all know exactly where I stand on women and their manipulative ways.

CHAPTER TWO

HOLDING
OUT FOR
FOREVER
BLACKPATH MC BOOK THREE

K im...

I'm nervous as can be, but nothing is stopping me now. I have everything I need in my purse to fulfill my mission tonight. I reach in and take one of the condoms out and put it in my bra. Chief is not the type of man I am used to dealing with. He's hard and a little too much like my dad and Kylar for me to get too comfortable with him. He won't be as easy to manipulate as the boys I'm used to. I have been trying to just once in my life be put first in the Steel family, but it never happens. I thought once Kylar, the boy wonder, finally settled down, I would be put first, but no. He couldn't even do that right. Callie is a nice enough girl, but now the attention is on Kylar and her and that brat she's carrying. Yes, I know, I should be happy I'm going to have a niece or nephew, but that just means one more person I must share my dad's attention with. I'm not jealous, it's just supposed to be my time.

Keifer has his problems with the dynamics of the power in the club, but my problems are all personal. I'll help him as much as I can. Dad used to call me his little princess, but it was still the boys he gave all his attention to. I am an afterthought. Keifer and I have figured out ways for both of us to get what we want. We have agreed to stay out of each other's way and help distract Dad from finding out, until it's too late.

I thought I had finally come up with the perfect plan to get what I wanted. My last boyfriend was a big enough ass to help with that without even knowing. I knew he was a hothead. I played the damsel in distress, but instead of my dad helping, it was Callie. That bitch is tough and now Dad, Kylar, and Ma, think she walks on water. Put a brat in the picture and she's up there with a saint. Now she's with someone else. Yes, an answer to my prayers, but they won't let her go. Now everything is about getting Callie back. Proving Kylar is a better man. Ma and Dad are going out of their way to help and are getting things ready to have the brat half the time. So, some other man is fucking Callie, and she is yanking my brother around, and they still can't get enough of her. What does a girl have to do to get some facetime with my own family? Yes, I thought I wanted out of the Feral Steel MC life, but I thought my dad would make me come back. Well, if Callie wants my family, I will have hers. I am a woman, and the man Callie will always love the most is her daddy. I will play the available girl neglected by her family, worm my way into his heart, and show her exactly how it feels to see your family torn from you. Dad will go ballistic, but any attention is better than none. All the while Keifer will have time to work his plan. At least I have him. He is no fan of Callie. We will tear her out of our family one way or another. I have her snowed that I am her friend, but I will be her downfall from my family, permanently, right along with her own. She can stay in Colorado and keep Devil's spawn with her. If she's lucky, I will let her keep her new man, but if not, I might just take a shot at him, too. Now I must play my cards close to my vest and not let anyone in on anything I'm doing.

I'm sitting in my car waiting for Chief to get here. I can't believe he's making me wait. I hear a bike, look in my rearview, and yes, there is Chief. I start with the waterworks. After years of practice I can turn them on like a faucet. I take another look in the mirror, and yes, there goes the mascara. Perfect touch. He drives slowly up the drive, and I am out of my car and ready.

CHAPTER THREE

HOLDING
OUT FOR
FOREVER
BLACKPATH MC BOOK THREE

Chief...

As I make it up my driveway, I see Kim has made it. I don't even get my bike parked, and she's beside me. I can see she has started her waterworks already. She has done the same thing every time we've talked, and it doesn't amuse me. She thinks she's playing me, but she doesn't realize I have been played by someone a whole lot better at it than she is, and it didn't work for her, either. I don't say a word to her as she follows me to the house. I get in and disarm the security. Might as well get this over with.

"Darling, I don't know what your angle is, but if you want a piece of me, I'll damn sure give it to you. Just remember you're a willing hole for me to stick my cock in, and that's all you'll ever be to me. No relationship, no girlfriend, no dates, and sure as fuck no damn ring. I'll use you to get off, and then I'll use you to get to Steel and Devil. You'll never hear I love you from me, and I don't sugarcoat shit for no one." If she can't understand what I'm telling her, it's on her, not me. I'm not trying to hurt her, just being real and maybe shock her.

"Wow. No hello or why are you upset or anything, just straight to it. I'm up for what you're offering. You are one arrogant asshole thinking I would want anything more. I'm not some whiny little girl." That's what she says now, but she comes here with those fake-ass tears running down her face. She dried right up when I didn't act as if I was going to comfort her.

"Isn't that exactly what you're acting like with that black shit running down your face? I don't care what's going on, and you'll get no sympathy from me. You will get nothing from me but my cock, when I want to give it, only when I want to give it, and I will give it to whoever I want. We are not exclusive, and we are nothing to each other. Can you accept that because I won't change my mind? Any club whore could be before or after you." That is as plain as it gets. No gray areas.

"You are a total dick, aren't you? Why are you so mean? What have I ever done to you? I thought we had become friends. We've been talking for a while and I've been to your house a few times." Kim is still trying to play me. She's in way over her head.

"I don't need any more friends. I trust my friends. You, I don't trust. You have your own reasons for being here, but tonight is all I'm offering. Not even all night, only until I have what I want, then you'll leave." Kim is biting on her bottom lip and I know she's trying to get to me. I look her over, and she is a beautiful young woman. She has long dark hair put up on her head like Callie used to always do before she cut it. She has a tight short dress on that leaves little to the imagination. Her long legs seem to go on forever and those fuck-me heels make them look even longer. Her ass is round and tight, and her tits are more than a handful and on full display. She's not some anorexic looking girl, she has hips I could hold onto. Damn, I need to get my mind off her body and back to getting information. I try to adjust my growing cock to get more comfortable.

"I could take care of that slight problem, or not so little prob-

14

lem, for you." She's grinning at me and for some reason that pisses me off.

"Spit out what you want Kim. I'm not stupid. I know you're going to do nothing for free. What do you want?" I am losing patience. I try to calm down. I hate bitches that think they can control a man because they have a pussy.

"Okay. I need someplace to stay for a few days. Dad is being an ass to me. He ignores me most of the time, but if he's not, he tries to control my every move. He doesn't approve of anyone I date, so I thought I would give him something to really not like. You." This girl is devious. No there's more to it.

"You mean he wants to keep you away from the Deacons of the world. My girl was shot because of your choice in men. He was a real keeper." *See what happens when I poke around.*

"Callie wouldn't have been shot if she hadn't jumped in. That wasn't my fault." This bitch is jealous of my girl. If it hadn't been for Callie, Kat would have been shot. Kim isn't even thankful her ma didn't get shot.

"Why not go to Stone? Surly he doesn't still live with Kat and Steel. Don't women your age have friends in your own state? Why come all the way to Texas and why me? Surely there are some college boys to stick it to your dad. Didn't you get enough of Daddy's attention when you were growing up? I thought you used to be his little princess, and I thought you were fighting to get away from the biker life. I'm a damn biker!" Kim makes no sense at all. She wants her dad's attention, but she doesn't. This just keeps getting more interesting. I'm getting pissed at her games, but I must keep my head to get all I can out of her.

"I did want out of the Feral Steel biker life. Not necessarily all bikers. I know the college boys just aren't man enough for me. They either use me for a while or want to smother me. I just can't find the right kind of man for me around where we live.

They're all intimidated by Dad." She may have just told me part of the truth for the first time since we've been talking, but not the full truth.

"So, you think you should fuck your ex-sister-in-law's dad. Not very smart. Not only will Steel and Devil not like it, but Callie won't like it if you're my fuck mate for a night. She's very protective of her family. Do you want to take the chance of pissing her off because I pissed Steel off letting him know you came here to see me when we were in Colorado?" Not that I care about Steel, but I do care about Callie.

"I can handle my dad's temper and Callie can mind her own business. She has her life now with Dra. I wasn't hiding it from anyone me coming here. I know I'm followed everywhere. I don't see what the big deal is about us hooking up or whatever. I know my dad, or the Feral Steel MC don't intimidate you. So, do you think I could stay here for a few days? I'll be sure and show my appreciation in a way you will get plenty of enjoyment out of it." Kim walks over to me and rubs her hand up my arm. I grab her by the back of her head and I take her mouth in a way to let her know I am not a man to play around. She opens her mouth and I take her in a crushing kiss. Thrusting my tongue in fast to get her attention and then slow down and let our tongues mingle. She tastes sweet, but I know she is anything but. I reach down and grab her ass and crush her front to mine, grinding my cock exactly where she wants it. When she is panting for air, I firmly push her back and away from me. Then I walk to my refrigerator, get a beer out, twist the lid off, pop it in the trash and take a long drink.

"Is that what you want Kim? To be used like a whore? At least you're twenty-one and old enough to drink. That's more time than Devil gave my daughter before he used her." I slowly take a drink waiting for her reaction.

"I'll be using you as much as you're using me, so maybe you're

16

the whore. Now can I stay or not? It won't be very long." Kim is standing there glaring at me and still playing the game.

"Okay. You can stay, but I have my eyes on you. You don't fool me. You are just dying for attention, and you think you'll change my mind, but you'll find out you won't. I picked up on the dislike for Callie and my advice to you is keep it in check. I'm not your daddy and if you fuck with her, there will be consequences you will not like. While you're here, you will drop your panties or get on your knees anytime I say, just like any other slut. Are we clear?" I need to keep her here for just a little while to get more information. Friends close, enemies closer.

"I can live with that as long as I get off, too." Kim is licking her lips and looking at my hard cock in my jeans, which has a mind of its own, and won't go down. I know she thinks she's won.

"I didn't say that did I? Now get over here on your knees and suck me off." She moves the small distance between us and her hand goes to my belt. I remove her hand and undo my own belt. If she thinks because I'll let her service me she's in control, she is very wrong. I know I'm being a bastard, but she needs to learn I don't have anything for her, except for exactly what I say. I will use her, but I don't want to destroy her. I take her by the arm and walk over and pull a chair out from the table. I slowly unzip my jeans, not in a hurry for anything. I push my jeans open and let my cock out from the confines it has been fighting against. It's already hard as steel. I reach down and run my hand from the root to the tip and back. Slowly, enjoying the feel. He is ready for a hot wet mouth. I work myself a couple times, going over the head and working the cum around it. I sit down in the chair and lean back with my head going back enjoying myself. I look at Kim and she can't take her eyes off my cock and how I'm working him. She's licking her lips like she's hungry enough to take me at any second. I continue to work myself and enjoy her watching, but it's time to test her. I snap my fingers at her and

17

point my head toward my cock. She never hesitates. She's down in between my legs in a flash of a second and instead of my hard hands, I feel her running her tongue under and around the head of my engorged cock. She deepthroats me without any warning and it feels so fucking good. I am lost in the feeling, but still trying to watch her. She sets a pace that is making me lose all thoughts. All I can do is enjoy and feel. She takes her hand and grabs my cock by its root and keeps the rhythm her mouth has set. She goes down and takes most of me in her throat. I feel her gag a little as she comes back up and twists her head, so her mouth is rotating all the way up my cock, then she tightens her lips as she gets to the head. She doesn't hesitate to repeat it. Kim sucks like a pro. I feel her moving her hand into my jeans and her cupping my balls, massaging them. Damn, if she keeps this pace up, this isn't going to last very long. I can't let this end so soon. When she comes back up, I push her mouth off me and stand up. She stands in front of me and I take the front of her dress in each of my hands, ripping it off her. She never takes her eyes off me. I toe my boots off and slide my jeans and boxers off in one move. I pull Kim to me and crush her mouth with my lips. She opens for me and I own her in that kiss. I shove my tongue in, so our tongues entwine and fight for dominance. I reach down and grab her ass and she crawls up my body with her long sexy legs. God, I knew they would feel great wrapped around me. I need inside her pussy. I turn and back her over by the chair I just left, throwing it out of the way. I drop Kim on top of the table and rip her panties off to see a completely bare, beautiful pussy. I see she's wet. Kim is a dirty girl that gets off sucking cock. I lean her back with my hand on her tit. She still has her bra on, but I pull the cup down and play with her pebbled nipple. Rolling it between my fingers, I hear a moan escape her. I move my hand down her slightly rounded stomach. I do it slowly, feeling her arch her back. She wants my cock, but I am in control. Instead of running my hand down to her pussy, I widen her legs and rub my hands on the inside of her thighs. Up and down softly and slowly. I bend down and start at her knee and run my tongue from there up to where it meets the inside of her leg and then back down. Her back is coming off the table and her breathing is labored. I do it again, but when I get to the top, I gently suck and then lick her clit. Repeating it softly and gently. Then I move back down, and I give her soft kisses back up. Now she is palming her own breast. She is pinching her nipples. This is almost my undoing, but I want her to beg. I spread her pussy lips with my hands and lean closer and blow softly on the clit that is a hard nub. I give it a soft lick and cover it with my mouth and suck gently while teasing it with my tongue. Then I let go and move to her other thigh and start to repeat the slow tease.

"Please, Chief. I need you to fuck me. I need to come." Kim is breathless, and I know she's on the edge, but I don't give in to her. I lick, and I kiss until I'm the one needing inside her. I stand up and look for my jeans to get a condom, but Kim pulls one out of her bra cup. I sheath myself quickly and bury myself to the root of my cock, grinding into her pussy. I set a fast pounding rhythm. I feel the tingle run up my spine and my balls are drawn up tight. I know it won't be but a few more strokes until I come, so I take my thumb and rub Kim's hard clit. It isn't but a minute, and she's coming undone. I feel her pussy spasm around my cock. Pulling it in deeper, she feels like a vise made just for me. I ground in one more time and it feels so damn good, I growl as I come and I don't think it's ever going to stop. Damn!

"You do know how to fuck, don't you?" I smile at Kim and she looks like she is still coming out of her haze.

"Don't think I really got to participate much in the second half. You played my body, and it was damn good Chief. We could be good together." Wrong answer from her.

I back away from her slowly, pulling out of her. I move to the trash can, take the condom off and go to wash my hands.

"Aren't you going to help me up?" Kim is looking at me expectantly.

"No, I'm done for now. Take care of yourself and clean the table for me when you're done. I'm calling in a pizza and grabbing a shower." I know that has to sting, but that's the purpose.

"You can stay in the spare room until you give me a reason to pitch your ass out. Pick up around the house while you're here. You give me one problem, and you're gone. If I want you, I'll come to you. There'll be extra pizza tonight, but all the rest of the time fend for yourself. Stay out of my way, no guests, and don't bother to try to steal anything." I turn around and point to the little security camera in the corner and flip it off. "We just gave my security guy and probably half the brothers at the club a good show." That should have been enough to keep her here, so I can get more information. Kim is the type of female that if you're nice to her she leaves but be a dick to them and you can't get rid of them. She'll be around until she accomplishes what she came for. Hopefully, I learn enough before she does any real damage. With that I walk out of the kitchen and down the hall while texting my order into my favorite pizza place. They know my order and by the time I get out it'll be delivered.

CHAPTER FOUR

HOLDING OUT FOR FOREVER
BLACKPATH MC BOOK THREE

K im...

Fuck that asshole. I look straight at the security camera and smile. I finally sit up on the table and get off it. The only thing that makes this situation better is I know my plan is already in progress. That makes me happy. I know where Callie's old room is, so I walk right in and go to her closet and pull out a t-shirt, then I see some sweats folded on the top shelf and grab those, too. These will be snug but will do until I can get to my car and get my bags out. I knew Chief would finally give in. Not like I was really going to leave anyway even if I had to sleep in my car. I make my way to the guest room, time for a hot shower.

I turn the water on as hot as I can stand it and get under the steaming water. It feels good on my body. For an older guy, Chief is in good shape. He has rock solid abs and he doesn't have any body-fat I could see. He played my body like the experienced man he is. I'm tired of playing with the college boys I have been fucked by. They're more into getting themselves off and forgetting what I might need. I received more pleasure from the fuck we just had on the table than I have ever had. This is going to be way more pleasurable than I thought. I've never been with a man that could make me beg. I not only begged, I screamed his name, and I will again. He may try to act like some hard-ass, but he will soon be begging me.

I finish up my shower and I feel better than I have in a long time. Yes, there's something to be said about being with a man that knows how to please a woman. I have things I need to get done. I dress quickly, the sweats are made for a woman with very few curves. Callie is a girl, and she hasn't got her curves yet. I don't have that problem with her t-shirt. I walk out of the bathroom into the guest room, and I look around the sparsely furnished room. Just the basics. Neutral colors. Blah... I stay here for more than a few days and I'll have to put some color in here. I jump on the bed and it seems comfortable. No TV, radio, or even a clock. I get up and look out the only window in the room. You can see the backyard. Nothing special. I look around the room to see if Chief has any security cameras in here, but I don't see any. However, I didn't see the one in the kitchen, either. I should have known he would have this house wired with cameras. I think after Callie took off, he put them everywhere. If he'd had eyes on her, then he would have known something was up. Well, cameras may deter some people, but I know how to use them to my advantage. Those boys want a show, I can damn sure give them one. Then they can be distracted every time they see me. This isn't my first rodeo. I have been doing this shit since I was fourteen years old. I drove my dad's club brothers crazy until I was ratted out by Kylar.

Kylar has always been a thorn in my ass. Keifer is older and you would think he would be the one to always be on the straight and narrow. No. Kylar has always been our dad's pick. Stone was rightfully pissed when Kylar was voted in as Vice President. All Keifer got was Treasurer. He does know where all the money is though, and that has helped both of us at one time or another. Being the oldest the gavel should go to him, but that will never happen, and Dad just threw Kizzy to the wolves, instead of protecting her the way they do Callie. Even Ma slighted Kizzy by giving Kylar the family rings to give to his new bride instead of the oldest son's wife. I get even less respect. We are going to change that. When I bag Chief as an old man they will have to give me the respect I deserve. Dad wants to form a friendship with the BlackPath MC and I can help with that. Not Kylar. Yes, this can work out well for me, and then I'll rub it into the smug faces of both Kylar and Callie. Then I will be daddy's little princess again, until Keifer takes all his power, too. It's a win-win for me.

I feel my stomach protesting; it's time to eat. I wander out into the kitchen and I see a box of pizza that smells great. I open it up and I see Chief has left me three pieces of supreme, which is my favorite. I love the spice of life.

CHAPTER FIVE

HOLDING
OUT FOR
FOREVER
BLACKPATH MC BOOK THREE

C hief...

I walk into the club at 5:45. I have fifteen minutes to grab a quick drink and get ready for church. We have a lot to cover. Everyone will be here. I motion for Joy to get me a beer and she's quick to get it to me. I barely slow down to pick it up. I know Jeb's cut is in my office and I need to pick it up. I'm trying to get my thoughts in order. Just as I am about to go down the hall to my office, Sas steps out in front of me. She tries to run her hand up my chest, but this shit is not happening. I need to nip this in the bud right now. "Get your fucking hands off me. Did I tell you to put your hands on me, bitch?" I am looking at her like she's a piece of shit I want out of my way, and I do want her out of my way. She's no better or worse than any of the other women that have become club girls or hang-arounds. She just needs to learn her place. We don't tolerate trouble in our club from pettiness.

"Come on, Chief. I haven't had that cock of yours in a while. Can't I help you get rid of some pent-up aggression? You look like you're tense." She is twisting the ends of her hair around her finger like some kid and I shove her other hand off me.

"Sas, this is a warning, the only one you'll get. You are a whore and nothing else. You serve your purpose, but you are nothing more than that. You don't own my cock. If I want to have Lita suck my cock in front of you, I will. That includes any woman I see fit. If I want to bend one over, right here in the middle of my club, I will. The next time I hear of you confronting another woman over me, you are barred. Are we clear, bitch?" I'm being loud and getting right in her face. She doesn't answer fast enough for me. "I can't hear you. Answer!"

"Okay. I understand." I can barely hear her. She's looking around to see who is listening.

"I still can't hear you!" She looks me in the eye and sees exactly how badly she fucked up.

"Yes Chief, I understand. I will cause no more trouble." She's looking at her feet, but I need to know she really understands, because I have no time for this shit.

"I expect you to apologize to Lita for confronting her, and Jeb for having to throw you out. In fact, you apologize to Lita in front of me after church." I leave her there looking at the floor. *Was it extreme, yes? Do I care, no?*

I go into my office and grab the box Kelsey left on my desk. I look at my watch and know I need to get to the big auditorium where we hold church. I get there just in time to see Brain making his way over to ZMan, who is busy taking everyone's piece until we're done. He and I are the only two left with our guns and phones. I see Jeb standing on the other side of the big doors, waiting like we asked him to.

I walk around them and over to the big table we sit around. I see everyone is here except Hambone, and he's come up behind Brain. I look at the big clock on the wall and pick up my gavel and bring this meeting to order. ZMan shuts the door and joins us at the table. I stand at the end of the table, so I can take care

25

of the first piece of business. "Okay. Everyone knows Jeb hasn't been prospecting for us a year yet, but he has proven his loyalty and he saved my slow ass from taking a bullet when we were in Colorado trying to square Callie away, so I want a vote for his patch." I look to Driller.

"I vote yes." Driller smiles, he has been wanting this.

"Yes." Tazer was one of the last ones voted in and he wants Jeb in as bad as Driller and I do.

It makes its way all the way around the table, and it's unanimous

"ZMan will you get him. Might as well get his vote for the remaining issues." He opens the door and motions for Jeb to come in. We knew how the vote would go. I motion for him to come over to me. "Jeb you have become a brother who is as dependable and loyal as anyone here. We voted, and you are now a BlackPath MC member. Congratulations Brother." I pat him on his back and hand him his cut out of the box I brought in. As I hand it to him, he notices I had a name put on it. "Yes brother, I have given you your road name, Shield. Seems fitting and I knew it would be yours since Colorado." He has a big-ass smile on his face.

"Thank you. Thank all of you. I will die before I let a one of you down or dishonor the BlackPath MC." He is treating his cut with the respect it deserves. Yes, he is a terrific addition and we need ten more just like him. "I like the name." All the brothers are congratulating him, but I know we must move on. So, I bang my gavel.

"We can all drink to it later. You have an appointment tonight to get our ink." I am very proud of how far he has come along. "Okay, let's get down to it. Brain you have the floor. Bring everyone up-to-date and give us all some answers." I sit down in my chair and Shield finds his new place next to Tazer.

"I was able to get my hands on a copy of Diamondback's will. He does have a set of twin daughters at Lake Cypress close to Mt. Vernon in Northeast Texas. They live on a family horse ranch with their aunt. Mother deceased. A DNA test was done at their birth. As far as I can find out, he has never been in their lives, but has sent regular child support. The mother was a club girl and she left and returned to her family. She didn't want him to have an active role in their lives. Also, I found out his son Braun did leave when he found out Diamondback was going to orchestrate the shit with Callie. He strongly disapproved. He was an officer, but not sure which one. He reportedly lost that position when he left, but not his membership. They agreed on that and left the door open." He looks at me to see if I have any questions.

"I want a meeting with Braun. Find him and ZMan will set it up." I'd like to see what he has to say.

"I'll do that, but it's like he fell off the face of the earth. He has used no plastic, no phone that can be traced, or social media. I'll try to find some of his friends to watch. Someone has to be helping him." Brain always finds a way.

"What else?" I need to find Brain someone to help him. His workload keeps growing.

"Found the man driving the vehicle the night Callie was shot at. He was shot before I could bring him in. I do have a recording of our phone conversation where he did say Stone is involved. He wouldn't say anything else, but I had a meeting set up. He didn't show, but his body was there." I look and see Brain is pissed it didn't pan out.

"Everyone knows Kim is staying at my house." I look at all their faces and see most have seen the tape of us in my kitchen. Most have smiles on their faces. Especially Brain.

"She put on a show this afternoon in your guest room. Apparently, she likes her sex toys." Tazer has a shit-eating grin on his face. I know my boy. I need to shut that shit down.

"She knows the cameras are there. She's using that shit. Tazer do not go there. She has a pure black soul. She is eaten up by jealousy and greed. She hates Callie and I think her whole damn family, except Stone. I will bet she's helping him. Stone wants Feral Steel MC. I don't know what her angle is with me. I treated her like shit and she keeps coming back for more. She's after something." All my brothers are paying close attention. "When she's around, do not be distracted by her body, pay attention or you're liable to be pulling a knife out of your back. As you have seen, I fuck her, but I never turn my back on her. I push her, and she ends up telling me more by how she says something or what she doesn't say. She has a real hate for Baby Girl, but she's like her best friend to her face, and she hates Devil. Spoiled girl who didn't get enough of daddy's attention. I bet she was behind that shit that went down with Deacon or at least pushed him into it and got the bastard killed. Do not let her play any of you." *I can't express that enough.* "Let's move on, just watch that bitch carefully."

"That's about it from me except the thing with Sarge. He's operating, as far as we can tell, just like always. He's making no contact with Callie. That's the only other thing you had me working on." Brain sits back to relax now the attention is off him.

"Good job. Shield, if Brain needs any help, give it to him. You had some training when you were in the Marines, which may help." As much as we have going on it will take some of the pressure off just one brother. "If none of the ol' ladies are interested in keeping the club girls in line, then we need to put Joy on the payroll to do the job. We need to make sure they are regularly tested and are on birth control. The ones that stay here need to have a cleaning and cooking rotation. Joy has been here the longest and she pretty well has her shit straight. She'd get a weekly check and benefits. It's the least we could do. She'd be like a house mom of sorts. She'd be responsible to keep this shit with Sas from happening again." I look around the table.

"Kelsey is opening another shop up and really doesn't have the time right now. I barely see her as it is," Hambone is the first one to speak up. Kelsey has been one of the ol' ladies we go to, but she does have a full plate right now.

"Chelsea is helping Kelsey out and has enrolled in some classes at the college. She also keeps the bar stocked and has been helping when no one else is available." ZMan is right, I have been seeing more of her here and she always looks tired and is in a hurry with somewhere to be.

"Laurie is busy teaching and she would kill these bitches. I don't want her upset any more than she has to be because she just found out today she's pregnant. We don't want to take any chances since the last two pregnancies ended up in miscarriages." Driller has shocked all of us. Him and Laurie have been together a long time and she has been pregnant twice and lost them both. We had all begun to think they had given up. I am happy for my brother. I hope my niece or nephew makes it. I reach over beside me and slap him on the back. Everyone congratulates him. "We had given up and it just happened. We are cautiously optimistic." They'll make great parents.

"Okay, then let's vote on Joy. We have more than one thing to drink to." Our family keeps growing.

"I vote yes." Driller is smiling from ear-to-ear. It goes around the table and Joy gets the job.

"Hammer how are our finances?" He smiles, and I know our businesses are booming. We don't have to do the illegal jobs we used to. We have legal booming businesses. We hire in-house as much as we can to keep trouble down, and we do good business.

"Six figures in the black with payroll taken off. I have some leads on some new venues and will give a full report when I have a chance to check them out. Each of you have detailed spread-sheets sent to you." We are doing well and growing. Hammer is a genius when it comes to business ventures, and he can smell a con a mile away.

"Any other business we need to tend to tonight?" I look at each of their faces and I see nothing but anticipation for some drinking tonight.

"I have just a couple more things. One, Baby Girl will be here in less than two weeks for a doctor appointment. The ol' ladies are planning something for her. When you speak to her, pay atten-tion to anything she says about Dra's club. Not that they are doing anything, and I don't care about interactions in their club. It's about Callie having extra security on her. Something is up, and I want to take no chances with her or my grandchild's safety. I know if I start asking questions of Dra or Hawser they will get pissy about it being their club business, and Callie is loyal to a fault and won't say anything, so just pay attention. Second, Shield I know I asked you to help Brain, but when you're not I want you and Tazer to take over the role of enforcers for now. I just feel like a shit-storm is coming our way with Diamondback, and this hate thing with Stone. ZMan will need your help, and you two are the most qualified. The three of you work like a well-oiled machine together. Killman is your backup. Get together and do some training. I think that needs a vote, too." I wait for Driller.

"I vote yes." Driller looks a little relieved. I imagine it'll take some pressure off him.

"I vote yes," Shield speaks up next. It goes around the table and once again is unanimous.

"Hambone, can you get Kelsey to do those patches when she has time?" Hambone nods affirmatively.

"Okay boys let's drink one to Shield getting voted in and Driller's great news." I slam the gavel down, but Driller stands, and I know he has something to say.

"The news of Laura being pregnant is not news everyone knows, so we want it kept quiet just in case. Just for a little while." I know this has him filled with fear, but we will all be here for support.

"Did everyone hear? Don't talk about it until they're ready." I give Driller a head nod. He knows he has us.

We all make our way to the bar and I see Sas on one side of the room and Lita on the other. I catch Sas's eye and nod towards Lita. I move within hearing distance and Sas does apologize. That's what I wanted, so it's done. Maybe all is settled, and we'll have calm for a while.

I move to the bar and nod at Joy to bring me a beer. "Joy we have a job opening for you. If you take it, you will be like a club mom. You'll take care of the bar, keep the girls squared away, and keep up with medical issues. You won't be considered a club girl anymore, but like family. You'll get a paycheck and benefits. Are you interested?" I see she's happy.

"Thank you, Chief. If the numbers are what I can live on, then yes. I can quit the lame jobs I have now." Joy seems excited at the thought of the new job.

"You can stay here in one of the rooms if you want so you don't have to pay rent." Then she'll be here if there's trouble with one of the girls.

"I want the job, but I need to keep my apartment until my sister gets on her feet, but then I'll take the room if it's still available." I didn't even know Joy had a sister. "My baby sister moved in with me about a month ago. She just moved here from Pittsburg. Her husband was killed in Afghanistan three years ago, and she's just surviving, not really living. She moved here to get a fresh start."

"I thought you were a Texas girl. What was your sister doing in Pennsylvania?" Joy had me curious.

"Oh no. She's from Pittsburg Texas. No h on the end. It's a very small town. She's twenty-six and she married her high-school sweetheart. She's a good girl and used to be crazy as hell, but when she lost Michael her light went out. I'm helping her get back to life even if she fights me at every turn. I was going to ask if I could bring her around, but she's really shy." I can tell Joy really loves her sister.

"What's her name? Joy you can bring her around but wait until we have something for family. You take this job and you'll be included in all our family functions. You said she's shy, so it would probably work better." I can't imagine another Joy that's shy. Joy is anything but shy.

"Her name is Emily. Em to most. You're right, a family function is better. I just want her to get back out there. Michael is the only man she ever even dated." Joy stops talking and looks like she's in thought and then she smiles. "Thank you Chief, for this chance. I won't let the club down." She has tears in her eyes.

"You deserve it Joy. You've shown your loyalty and you've been here over ten years with no problems. Just keep a strong hand on these females. All we need is fighting in our club. I have no patience for it. Now be sure everyone is happy tonight and get with Hammer for the paperwork. If anyone gives you shit, let me or ZMan know." I see Shield raising a shot glass and I know he's on his way to a great party, but I'm just tired, so I head to my room for some much-needed rest. I sleep with one eye open in my house.

CHAPTER SIX

HOLDING OUT FOR *FOREVER*
BLACKPATH MC BOOK THREE

C hief...

The last two weeks have been a whirlwind. Callie is here, and I am going to go wake her soon, but I just need a few minutes to really take in having my daughter back home, even if it is temporary. I should be able to get some sleep tonight.

Just when I thought we would get everything under control and tie up loose ends, we found out another club is pushing drugs. That shit doesn't happen in our town. We are busy on all fronts now. We will put this club out of our town with a quickness.

My mind goes to my other problems. I came home two nights ago to find Kim gone. Apparently, Steel is under the impression Kim and I are more than we are. He called and said if we stayed together, it was full out war. The next day she's gone. He threatened Callie's freedom. I told him to fuck off, but where he got the impression Kim and I are anything is beyond me. I couldn't help but to let him believe it for now. Now he knows how it feels. Kim's playing her games. Not that I want her here, but something has changed; I don't know what and I don't like it. I think it's time for a little chat with Devil. I will let him decide what to tell Steel. I also need to call Dra and have a talk with him. He needs to be aware of the threat to his ol' lady. This isn't easy for me, but the more I think about it, the more I know it's the right thing to do. Realizing Callie is a full-grown woman with an old man to take care of her is not easy, at all. Devil is my grandchild's father and it's his right to be able to know about Kim's hate. This shit is making me feel old. I won't ever let my baby girl completely go, but I must give respect to the men in her life, because if it was the other way around I would go ballistic. My mind is set.

I get up and get my shower. It's still early, but everyone needs to get a move on. Today we find out if Callie is having a boy or a girl. I would love to have a little granddaughter but will love either one. Just want it to be healthy.

I also have to deal with Blake. I didn't know Blake was coming but am glad Callie didn't make that trip alone. Blake said he has plenty of vacation time, but I know his boss is trying to get rid of him. Another thing that needs taken care of. We need to finally settle our differences. I know it's time.

My house is full again. It has felt empty since Callie has been gone. Before it was always full of laughter and her friends, but now it's just a place to sleep, when I do that. I've spent more time here since Kim has been here. That could be because all we do is fuck while I pump her for information. No, that didn't make it feel like a home. It just made it feel lonely. Damn, I need to get Callie up and run to the clubhouse.

I make my way to Callie's room and knock. "You better get up sleepyhead. You'll be late for your doctor appointment. Today is the big day." I sure am excited about that. It takes me back to when Cheryl was pregnant with Ty.

"Okay, Dad. I'll shower and be down to cook." Finally, some of

34

her good home-cooking. "Dad it's still early. Everything okay?" Callie always knows. She's too smart for her own good.

"Just life, Baby Girl. I need to run to the club, so thought I would wake you first. Can't say I haven't missed your cooking, and I am looking forward to it." My stomach could do with it. It's already growling.

"Okay, it'll be ready when you get back." I turn and leave, knowing I need to get this done and get back. My phone call to Dra won't wait, and there's no way I want Callie to hear it.

CHAPTER SEVEN

HOLDING
OUT FOR
FOREVER
BLACKPATH MC BOOK THREE

Kim...

"Look who I found outside." Ty is cute as hell, but dumb as a bag of rocks. Like Callie can't see who we are.

"Well good. Food is almost done." Callie is fixing another of her fattening, heart-attack-waiting-to-happen breakfasts again. Has the woman never heard of healthy food? Blake goes over and kisses Callie. How sickening. Women do not get kissed on the forehead by uncles at her age.

"Good morning, sweetheart. Look at you. You look beautiful, pregnant and in the kitchen." Ma is fussing over the fat cow. "I have missed you." I don't want to be here, but I need to be. I need to turn that knife I placed in Chief's heart when I left with no word. He tries to act like he isn't affected, but I know he is. All he has to do is realize it, and what better way than to put myself under his nose as the dutiful friend. Even my family swallows it and they have known me forever. I can't believe Chief didn't set my dad straight when he called the other night, but Chief's hate for my dad is working to my advantage.

"Don't know about beautiful, but I'm comfortable." *Could Callie ask for more attention?*

"You're very beautiful barefoot and pregnant in the kitchen. Would only be better if it was my kitchen." *Could Kylar grovel anymore?* He might as well cut his balls off and let Callie carry them around. He's not a MC VP, he's a worm. If these people slobber over Callie anymore, I'm going to throw up. He even went as far as to wear the cologne I helped her pick out for him. Since he can barely function these days, it's hysterical. Much more and Stone won't have to take over the MC, they will hand it to him. I decide to completely tune out, so I don't have to hear anymore, until I hear Chief and Driller come in the door. Chief is pissed, and I can tell it has to do with me. Exactly the reaction I wanted. I'm getting to him. It'll be no time before he's crawling to me and begging. He's trying his best to keep his eyes off me, but I know he's paying attention. He goes to get a cup of coffee.

"Everyone ready to eat? We have about forty minutes until we need to leave." He wants out of this room. I smile at him sweetly. No reaction. He fixes himself a huge plate. "I'll be in my office. Come get me when you're ready." That's it. He walks out. Ty and Driller follow close behind. Probably has work to talk about. Then I notice Callie is giving me an evil look as if she's trying to see if she can see inside me. Her little friend Felix is doing the same thing.

"Anyone want to explain what just happened? Because I will not have my dad thinking he has to go to another room to eat in his own house." I look at Kylar. Apparently, no one has let Callie know everything that's going on. Interesting. I thought they let her in on everything.

"I told you I should have stayed at home." I give the most help-less act I can. Yes, I have put Dad on the warpath. Ma pats my arm trying to reassure me. I stare at my brother.

37

"Steel told Chief if he stayed with Kim it would be full out war. Chief told him to fuck off, but when Steel talked to Kim, she went back home. To say the least, Chief was pissed, but when he found out he threatened your freedom, Chief lost it." Blake just needs to let everyone know. Everything is going just the way I want it. Now the bitch will feel guilty. Or that's what I thought her reaction would be. Then I see her reach for the phone.

"Steel. What the hell do you think you're doing? I will say this one time only, so listen, no one uses me against my dad. Now I'm going to tell you, find another way. I don't care if you tie your damn daughter down. I don't care if you put a damn moat around your house, so you can keep her there. Do not use me!" Callie is pissing Dad off and I have to give her props for not backing down from all the yelling. " No, you shut up and listen to me; you have thirty minutes to change your tactics. Yes. By the time I leave to go to the doctor's appointment, my dad better have received a phone call from you, letting him know whatever you think you have on me has disappeared. Are we clear? If he doesn't, with everything in me, you will never lay eyes on this child. Do you get that you overgrown brat? Find another way!" I can't believe Callie just lit into my dad that way without hesitation. He will never cave to her demands, and I will be the good daughter because I listened to him and went home. She has her nerve speaking to him that way. I want to hurt her. Then my sniveling brother is looking at her like he's going to apologize for Dad. I better try to smooth this over, so she thinks I'm still on Chief's side.

"I'm sorry. I love your dad, but I don't want you in any trouble. Dad still has some things on you about the night that dumbass tried to take me." That sounded sincere. She looks like she bought it, but something in Kylar's eyes looks skeptical. Surely Dad didn't tell him that I said they should take a hard stand with Callie. I know I was taking a chance saying that to Dad, but he wouldn't have told Kylar. Callie is looking at my ma.

"I tried to talk reason into him. He's going crazy over Chief with Kim. He will do anything. All the men in our family have lost their good sense. First Kylar and the crap he pulled with you Callie, and now this. I'm at the point I am going to disown every damn one of them. You do what you have to. I love them all, but enough is enough." Ma is being disloyal again. She already made Dad stay at the clubhouse for weeks, and they fight all the time. She doesn't deserve our family. Sometimes I wish Deacon had shot her and maybe then she would realize who family really is. Now she's just sucking up to Callie. I'll make them both pay.

CHAPTER EIGHT

HOLDING
OUT FOR
FOREVER
BLACKPATH MC BOOK THREE

Chief...

I couldn't stand to stay in the kitchen and see Kim's face any longer. She kept following me with her eyes, waiting for me to speak with her, but it's not happening until I can control this anger. I spoke with Dra on the phone, so he knows about Kim, but he seemed distracted. He's going to keep a close eye on Callie. I also let him know about Diamondback's other children and he wants to keep it from our girl until after the baby is born, or until Diamondback comes clean. He's trying to protect my girl, so I must agree with him. She hasn't known about them for this long, so a little while longer isn't going to hurt.

I must be sure to get Devil off by himself before he goes back home. This shit with Steel needs to be handled. I have other things to concentrate on. ZMan says another high school student has overdosed on that shit that's being sold on our streets. It must end before anyone else gets hurt. We must stop the Possessed Blood Soul MC.

Tazer and Driller are staring at me. Driller finally decides to speak. "Are you going to let them know what's going on? I mean Devil, Callie, and Kat? They have to think you're sulking over Kim leaving."

"One damn thing, grown-ass men don't sulk. I am going to speak to Devil when I can get him off by himself. That's hard to do since Dra isn't here to keep him from sniffing around Callie. It'll be his nose up her ass all day. I won't ruin today for Baby Girl." I'll figure out a way. We'll be lucky not to come to blows, but at least he'll be warned. I have noticed a change in Devil. He's trying to do right, but we'll see. "I spoke with Dra about their situation, as well. Since Colorado has legalized marijuana, there has been some growers who want some land and a house Hawser has. He doesn't want to sell, and they've been giving the Troubled Fathoms problems. That's why Dra has the extra security on the women. Dra said it's their club business, not ours, and they have it handled. That's the same thing Brain dug up, so we just need to let it ride out and hope for the best. Hopefully, if they can't handle it, they'll ask for the help I've already offered. Callie doesn't know about it all, so no slip-ups."

"After the baby is here, I'm setting up a meeting with Callie's siblings. I'll give Diamondback that long to come clean about it. By then Dra will be on board, too." I don't like keeping secrets too long, they always bite me in the ass.

"Baby Girl is going to be happy. She always wanted a sister. She wanted you to shack up with someone and give her one." Tazer is right. She will be happy.

"I love both of you, but I'd rather cut my nuts off than raise another child in this life. I love my brothers, but club life is harder than hell sometimes and you miss so much being gone. You two were smart and learned your lessons fast, but to start all over? No, I'll leave that for the younger, more patient sorts." I look at Tazer and he understands. I missed a lot of ball games, hunting, and camping. I look at Driller and that poor bastard doesn't know what he's in for. I take my last bite of food when my phone goes off. I look at it—what does this hothead want? Steel and I said what there was to say a few nights ago. I flip open my phone to hear what the ass has to say.

"Yeah?" That's all I'll give him.

"Never took you for one to let women do your talking for you." *What the hell is Steel talking about?*

"What the hell are you going on about? No woman speaks for me." I am irate and rightfully so.

"Callie called me and gave me a fucking what for and threatened me with not seeing my grandchild like I'm doing something wrong." Steel must have gotten on the bad side of Baby Girl. I just don't know how she found out. It's time to enlighten Steel on a few things.

"How's that my problem? I haven't told Callie about the shit you said. I told you to fuck off and that was what I meant." I'm sure Callie is pissed.

"Look asshole, leave Kimberly alone. Then I'll leave Callie alone." This man is too much.

"You know what, the other night when you called I thought I would let you think what you wanted because you deserved it. Now I'm telling you. Kim means nothing to me. Never has. She came to me with her daddy issues and asked me for a place to stay. I gave it to her and I couldn't care less she's gone. In fact, I don't even want her in my house, but this is for my daughter, so whatever she's told you is a sack of shit. I care nothing for her." That's as direct as I can give it to him.

"So, you haven't fucked my daughter. You have no relationship, and this is just more of her drama?" Steel is grasping at straws. He knows no woman will ever be anything to me.

"We have no relationship. I did fuck her, seven ways to Sunday, but that's all it was. She offered more than once, and I took her up on it many times, but she's like any other whore to me." See how he likes that.

"You fucking motherfucker. That's my daughter you're talking about. We didn't disrespect Callie like that." Steel is furious and that is exactly how I want him.

"Oh, really? Using her to get another woman back. Making sure she got pregnant and then abandoning her. At least when I fucked Kim, I was smart enough to wear a condom and she knew exactly what we were. I didn't lie to her about anything and I told her where she stood with me. She not only agreed to it, she wanted it. Now this conversation is about over since you know your daughter is no better than a whore." I have now avenged the use of my daughter.

"Tell Callie she wins." With that Steel disconnects. I laugh. Baby Girl strikes again.

"Well that was brutal. Is he looking for blood?" Tazer knows I would be if the shoe was on the other foot.

"No, actually Steel sounds defeated. He can't deny what a shit job he did raising his children and the way they've turned out. I need to set Callie straight about doing things behind my back." *She must stop. She's going to be a mom soon.*

"Like that's going to do any good." Tazer is right, but I get up and head to the kitchen on a mission. It doesn't take me long to get there.

"Baby Girl what the hell did you do? I can take care of Steel myself." She needs to know to let it go.

"Taking care of business, Dad. No one uses me to hurt you. Not even Steel." I go over and give Callie a big hug.

"Callie is on the warpath again." Driller is smiling from ear-to-ear. He's loving this.

Kim walks in from outside. "Dad is mad, but he won't use anything against Callie. I guess that means I can stay if you want me." This woman is delusional. I told her if she left not to come back, and she thinks this changes things. I don't even want to talk to her. She just keeps looking at me.

"This changes nothing between us. I told you if you left you weren't coming back, and I meant it." I turn my back to her and look at my watch. "We need to get moving."

Callie is riding with Fe and everyone else just gets into their own vehicles. The ride didn't take too long, and Devil and Callie go to the back first, while we are left to sit up front. Good thing today is not a busy day, or this would be one crowded room. Kim keeps trying to make eye contact and it's not happening. She can leave today and never come back. Kat keeps giving me the eye; if she keeps it up she will be enlightened just like her husband was on her daughter's antics. Soon they call us all back and we each step in long enough to see the sonogram and hear the heartbeat. There is not a more beautiful sight or an amazing sound. I am going to have a grandson. I am over the moon. I can do some of the things I missed out on with Ty. We give both congratulations and as soon as I see the baby on that screen, I know another piece of my black heart has been claimed. I will do anything to protect that baby. Not like before I wouldn't have but being able to finally see him again just cemented it.

We are out of the doctor's office and heading back to the clubhouse. The ol' ladies all want to visit with Callie and see the sonogram pictures. I know Devil will be there until we chase him out, so I should get a chance to talk to him. I know Kat is talking with Kelsey about baby showers. *Who would have ever thought baby showers would be discussed in our clubhouse?*

As soon as we are inside all the ol' ladies have Callie cornered and she's showing the sonogram pictures off. Kat is being the proud grandma-to-be and showing hers off, too. I watch as Kim looks on. She has a look of hatred in her eyes. I grab Devil by the arm and I nudge my head towards the group. "Watch the look on your sister's face towards Callie. Does that look like a friendly look to you? Now make your way to my office, we need to have a little talk and then you can decide what you want to tell Steel." He looks at me but moves towards my office. I nod at Driller and ZMan to follow. Then I notice a beautiful woman I have never seen before behind the bar helping Joy stock it. She is one hot piece of ass. She has curves, not like some of the anorexic looking women around here. She has low-slung jeans that hug her plump ass and her tits are amazing. I nod my head at her and she smiles and blushes. Well damn. I give her a little wink and her eyes hit the floor. Yes, I will be getting to know her. I know I must get in there with Devil, but I look over at the huddle of ladies and I see Kim staring at me. Her eyes then cut to the woman I was just checking out, and she already has a hate for this unsuspecting woman. I stare Kim down. She finally lets it go and looks away. I give the woman one more look and go to my office.

I close the door as I walk in. They all look at me and then each other. None of us thought we would ever be having a sit-down again. I've been thinking on how to approach Devil. There are only a few things he loves more than the Feral Steel MC. Callie and his soon-to-be-born son I assume are at the top of the list. I have to think he would go to the ends of the earth to protect them even if he's crazy about it at times. I hate to think he loves my daughter, but why else would she drive him to the edge of insanity? I've been there once-upon-a-time, so I know what it looks like. I walk around my desk and sit in my chair without saying a word. Then I just look at Devil.

"Do you still love my daughter? Do you love your son? Because I want you to keep that in mind as I tell you a story of deception and what the ramifications could be to them if you go off half-cocked. Don't let your rage or outrage react without thinking. Can you do this?" I stare him in the eyes waiting for his answer.

"What are you talking about? Is there something happening I need to know about because no one fucks with my family. Tell me Chief." I believe him, but I still need to remind him.

"Only your son is your family. Callie belongs to someone else. Remember that Devil." If looks could kill, I would be dead now.

"Just spit it the fuck out! If there is something going on, I have a right to know. She's carrying my child." I believe him. I also believe he will do what it takes to keep the peace. I look at Driller and ZMan and I see they agree.

"Devil, your sister is playing dangerous games. She has a lot of hate inside her for a lot of people. In fact, I would say the only person she really is partially honest with is Stone. Who, by the way, is also up to no good." I wait for his response, but I see he doesn't want to believe anything I'm saying. Then I see a smirk come across his face.

"I don't want to get dragged into any he said, she said, shit. I told Kim to stay away from you, but she wouldn't listen, so if this is to get back at her for leaving, forget it." I thought Devil was smarter than this.

"Do I look like I have turned into a man that has turned into a crying bitch? I was up front with Kim about the relationship we would have, which is none. I don't do fucking relationships. Ever. I told her she would be like any other bitch I fucked, and if you would like to see a recording of that, I have it on security tapes. I repeated it over and over. I just warn you that I am fucking your sister on these tapes, and after the first one, she knew about it and put on more than one show for my brothers all by herself and smiled while she did it. Now do I have your attention?" I see when he realizes I'm telling the truth. I remember the little story she gave me about teasing the men of her dad's club and Devil knows that, too.

"Okay. Just tell me." Devil is biting his tongue.

"Kim has a jealousy so hard for Callie I'm surprised she can even be around her, and the same for your son. She doesn't get enough of Daddy's attention. She wants to be front and center at any cost. I don't know what she wanted with me, except to make your dad pissed. Her and Stone have something cooking, but she left before I could get all the information. We also found out Stone is the one responsible for the shooting outside of the club the night all of you were shot at. You've got shit going on in your club and no one is paying attention. Take care of it, or we will. We have no concrete evidence to show or Stone would be in the ground already. I believe if you look into the books you will find out he has sticky fingers, too." Devil wipes his hand down his face.

"All I can say is we are aware, and we will take care of it as soon as we have evidence that's for sure. He's our blood. We're trying to give him enough rope to hang himself, and that's all I'll say. That's more than I should have, but I know you're concerned for how it will affect your daughter." At least I know they aren't completely stupid.

"Why didn't you come to me when you found out Stone might have had Callie shot at? You want me to keep you up-to-date, but you do nothing to make me think I can trust you. We found out about Stone on our own, and if you would just watch Kim, you would see the hate coming off her. I will not hesitate putting either one to ground for trying to hurt Callie." They have had time to put both Stone and Kim in check.

"All I can say is we're aware of Stone, but we take care of our own business. Kim has always been spoiled, but we didn't know

47

they were working close together. I won't let them hurt my son, or Callie." I almost believe him, but I must be sure. Devil is unpredictable.

"I'm putting you on notice; if we come up with evidence that for sure links Stone to the shooting, he will be dealt with. I won't give notice; it will just happen. I've also heard he's planning on taking over the Feral Steel. That means he would have to get rid of you and Steel, so watch your backs. Kim is out of my bed and house, and she won't be let back in. Keep her away but watch her. She's nowhere near the person she pretends to be, and Dra and I will be having a talk with Callie as soon as your son is born. Until then, all of us have an eye on her. Are you understanding what I'm saying?" I need to make sure he completely understands. "I'm sure she had something to do with Deacon going after Kat. That means she has no conscience."

"Chief, I understand. I don't think Kim would do that, but I will keep an eye on her. Stone I don't trust at all, but he will be dealt with by us, not you or the BlackPath MC." Devil better be smart, or he'll find himself in more trouble than he can handle. You need to watch your six in our lifestyle, or you will find yourself dead.

"Our intel is good. We know Stone isn't going to wait until you and Steel are ready, to try a takeover. Just watch your back." Driller is trying to get Devil to see the chance they're taking in waiting instead of acting.

"Dad has to give Stone a chance. It will be hard to handle for everyone, but especially Ma. We will take care of it. If that's all, I'm going to join Callie." We all knew this was going to be hard. In fact, I wouldn't want to be in Steel or Devil's shoes, but I would do what was best for the BlackPath MC. We all know when we put on a cut the consequences of betraying our colors, our brothers, and the club we pledge to. Stone's foot is already one step in hell and he doesn't even know it yet. Devil makes his way out the door.

I sit back in my chair, mulling over everything that has been happening and I know things are going to be interesting for the next few months.

"What do you want us to do about Kim?" ZMan is as apprehensive about her as I am.

"Just watch her while she's still here. Do you know who the woman is that was helping Joy?" I haven't been able to get her completely out of my mind. A woman her age usually doesn't blush. I'm guessing her age at around twenty-five.

"That's Em. Joy's little sister. She was helping stock and clean up today." Driller smiles as he says it. "I knew she would catch your eye."

"Have to be blind not to see her. She was behind our bar. I just didn't know who she was." Joy didn't say her sister was so beautiful.

"She's shy though. The times she has been around, the only person I've heard her talk to is Joy and that isn't much. Do you think she thinks she's too good to talk to us?" ZMan doesn't cotton to people he can't figure out, and if she's not talking he won't be able to figure her out.

"Joy said she was very shy, so that's probably it. Just give her some time but do a background check on her anyway. Better safe than sorry with a new MC trying to come in." You can never be too safe. Then I hear a commotion coming from the hall and we're out the door.

What I see when I get there has me speechless. Emily has a man I've never seen on the floor in an arm lock. His nose is bleeding and she looks about ready to kill him. ZMan makes his way over and takes Em's place before I can say anything. "What the hell is going on? JOY!" I yell for Em's sister.

"Damn Em, what are you doing?" Joy looks surprised.

"I caught him trying to put a package in the storage closet and when I asked him about it he grabbed me and said he was going to let me escort him out the back door. I knew he wouldn't let me go, so when I got to the hall I punched him in the nose with my elbow and kneed him in the balls. We wrestled out here to the hall, and then everyone else showed. He doesn't have a vest on like the rest of the men, so I didn't know if he belonged or not. I'm sorry if I did something wrong but he was acting suspicious. I would still check that box. He was sticking it under the bottom shelf and he put a box in front of it." Em was bleeding where it looked like she busted her lip. I looked at the man on the floor again and I didn't recognize him, but I wanted to break him in two for laying hands on Em. I feel very protective of her, and I don't like it. Joy was by her sister trying to wipe her lip off. Everyone from the front room had come to the hall, but I didn't see Baby Girl or Devil, I did see Kim, however.

"Tazer check on Callie." I don't know what's going on, but I want eyes on her.

"Devil took her back to the house because she wanted a nap. They're going to be back later." Good, he'll take care of her.

I nod my head at ZMan, so he'll get the man up. "Shield go check the package. Em show him where it is." I look the man over. I have to fight the urge to kill him. "Who are you and what are you doing here?" Shield has made it back in and he's handling the package carefully.

"I'm not saying shit. Do your worst. You're getting nothing." I see Kim and she's trying to get closer. I know she's trying to hear what's going on.

"Driller get everyone back in the bar area. In fact, everyone but members and family, out period. Have Hambone drive Kim and Kat to my house and stay there until I get there. Tell them to keep this quiet. I'll text Devil to make sure it's kept that way, and not to tell Callie. She doesn't need to worry." I move towards Em and put my hand at the small of her back to guide her into my office along with the man, ZMan, Shield, and Tazer. I shoot Devil a text and tell him not to leave Callie alone and to keep his mouth shut. The first person I see is Blake and he's watching close as he enters my office with Joy following behind him.

"You here as a lawman or as family? You know where I stand on it." Blake stands beside the man and looks him over.

"I'm a lawman, but I am concerned for my family and it's about time I start acting like it. If that's a bomb, Shield may need my help." I had thought about that, but I must make sure Blake is here as a friend and not an enemy. I look at the man Blake has become. We were at one time as close as brothers. Him, Tommy, and I were all best friends. I have missed him, but he's the one who took another road to get to his destiny. I wanted revenge for Tommy's death and he wanted justice. It was the start of a rift between us, but he is still my friend Blake. I know he would lay his life down for me and me for him, but there are so many mistakes and misunderstandings on both sides. I want him back in my life, but not at the expense of the BlackPath MC. "I'm here as your oldest friend and I'm a big enough man to apologize for my mistakes." That's all I needed to hear.

"You'll do it in front of the club?" I wait for him to decide.

"Yes. Now let me check the damn package before it explodes." I nod my head and both him and Shield start examining the package. "Can the club go through a search warrant if necessary? Anything you need to get rid of?" I know he's just being careful.

"We are clean. No one sells anything illegal here. We are legit all

51

the way." Blake shakes his head at Shield. They open the box and take out two rolled bundles of a white substance sealed in plastic. *Someone has spent a lot of money trying to set us up. If they took this big of a chance, then they're desperate to get us out of the way. The man here doesn't look nervous at all. Meaning he's either stupid, or he knows nothing.*

"Joy take Em to your room here and stay until everything is handled. I don't want either of you leaving until we check everything out." *I look at Em and she's as white as a sheet.*

"I know your club didn't have anything to do with whatever that stuff is." *I didn't realize I cared what she thought, but I feel relief as she says it.* I nod my head at her and Joy takes her hand and they leave.

"How do you want to handle this Chief? Your call. I can call it in, but your clubhouse will be searched, or we can search the club ourselves. I know you worked too hard to clean this club up to be dealing." *Well that surprises the hell out of me, but it's a good one.*

"Let's not get ahead of ourselves. We don't know it's drugs, it's just a white substance. If he doesn't want to cooperate, then we're going to let him test it. Blake what do you think it is?" *Now the man is getting antsy.*

"Tazer get a spoon and candle. Isn't that how druggies do their drugs? I don't know where we'll find a syringe, but maybe we'll just pour it down his throat and see what happens." *Driller raises his eyebrows. He may be a biker, but he hates needles. Every tattoo he's ever had he's nearly passed out from. He must really want the ink to do it.*

"I can see if Chelsea is still here. She may have an insulin syringe with her." *That did it. The guy is going to crack.* ZMan heads to the door.

"Man, you can't do that. Just turn me over to the cops. Someone paid me to sneak in here and put the box in the closet. They told me there would be deliveries today and a lot of people around and where the closet was. I have nothing against any of you. I'm sorry." Now we're getting somewhere, but we need more.

"Who the hell sent you? They had to know you might get caught. Even with a lot of people here, how did you get in?" He doesn't look like he wants to divulge the information. I nod to ZMan and he starts to open the door.

"Okay. I'll tell you everything I know. That is crystal meth and not even the good stuff. They just told me to stash it and where. They told me to be at the club gates at 6 pm sharp and there would be a distraction to get me in, and then leave when everyone started leaving. I got here, there was a distraction, and I got in, but that little bitch saw me. Now I'm going to die because I owed someone." He was practically sniveling on himself. Who the hell is on the gate and what kind of distraction?

"What was the distraction and who sent you?" I am running out of patience. He's stalling.

"Some bitch was giving the guard a blowjob. Kept him busy. The only thing I know is the guy called her Sas. All I saw is the back of her as I was slipping in."

That stupid bitch.

"The guy was tall, and he wore a vest sort of like the ones you wear, but different. I owed my bookie, and this was supposed to help pay my debt, but it's not worth dying over. I only saw the guy who dropped off the box once. He has long stringy dark hair and a long scar down his right cheek—like someone had sliced his face open with a knife. That's it. That's all I know." I don't know if that's all he knows, but I believe it's all he will give us. This guy needs to be iced until we can figure what to do with him, but first we need to get rid of these drugs before the cops do come knocking. I need to think, and he doesn't need to hear anything we say.

"ZMan tie his ass up and put him in our safe-room. Be sure to blindfold him so he doesn't see anything or knock his ass out." Tazer hands ZMan a bandana to blindfold him and Shield gets up and gets some rope from the storage closet in my office. After the man is blindfolded I realize we never got his name. "What's your name?"

"Orrin, Orrin Cox." I think the situation is finally sinking into his brain because he's shaking. ZMan takes him by his shoulder and leads him out with Shield following him.

"How the hell do we get rid of those drugs and what do we do with this guy?" I'm running all the options through my head and none are good enough. I flip open my phone and text Brain to get in here. "Blake are you sure this is drugs?" Blake comes over and cuts the plastic and smells it, licks his finger and dips the tip in the white substance. He barely sticks it to his tongue. I can't believe he did that shit. What if the shit was poisoned? "What the hell are you doing?"

"It's crystal meth. I do this for a living, remember? I can dispose of it for you. You don't just wash this shit down the drain." I look at Blake as if saying are you sure and he nods his head. "I'm sure, let me do it for the club, to make up for the hell I put it through with the doubts. Besides, I can do it safely. I have a friend that owes me a favor. I trust him, and it will only be on me."

"You're still a lawman Blake. What if you get caught?" Blake laughs.

"Don't worry, Chief. I don't plan on being a lawman much longer, and I know this was planted. It will do no good to call in the boys in blue. They'll just use it to their advantage and I don't want to see that happen. Besides, if your boys get rid of it, they are liable to dispose of it improperly and with this shit that can be dangerous." He's right about that. I know I should get a vote on this, but it needs immediate attention before we get busted.

"Can you take care of it now? I don't want it here any longer than it has to be." He nods yes and about that time there is a knock on the door and Tazer gets up and gets it. Brain walks in and is going to shut the door, but ZMan and Shield walk in. "Blake is going to dispose of this shit for us." Blake is cleaning everything up and putting everything in the box. I text Killman and Cutter to follow Blake and be sure everything goes off without any problems. He carries the box to the door and stops.

"Thank you for trusting me and letting me take care of this. I know it doesn't make up for what happened, but maybe it can help." Blake opens the door and hurries out. Damn this day keeps getting longer. My mind drifts to Em and I wonder how she's doing, but I have business to take care of now.

"Brain, the man we are looking for has long dark hair and a long scar on his right cheek. Do what you can to find him. Who was on the gate today at six?" Brain looks at his phone.

"Prospect Giles. He had from noon to eight tonight." He's a good kid, but he fucked up royally. He's young, but like all of us, he must show his loyalty by hard work. Brain moves around my desk and gets on my computer and starts working.

"Get him and Sas in here." Driller leaves to go get them.

"We need to search this club from one end to the other. We've gotten sloppy. If someone thinks they can sneak someone in and out without getting caught, then we have gotten lazy. It would have worked if it hadn't been for Em. She doesn't even know all of us and knew he didn't belong. Brain send a text out and get everyone here, let's get a search done now. We will have to vote on what to do with these two and Orrin. I'm sure Giles will just

55

walk, but I don't know about the other two." Sas has stirred shit up for the last time, turning on the club is the last straw. The only ones I can think of with drugs are the Possessed Blood Souls and they have out-stayed their welcome from day one. It doesn't take Driller long to get Giles in here and Driller has sent Sinner after Sas. I know Giles feels the anger rolling off me. I get right in his face. "Why the hell would you be getting sucked off while you have gate duty? I thought you wanted a cut like your dad?"

"Sas' car broke down outside the gate. It was just a loose battery cable and I tightened it and it started right up. She wanted to repay me. I told her to wait until I was off duty, but she insisted and well...I finally gave in. Why? Nothing happened."

"Asshat, it was a distraction, so someone could sneak in, and they did. You know the fucking rules. Your dad has gone to get Sas, and you both will pay for this. You were played for a fool." Sinner didn't even say anything to take up for his son. "Go out and sit at the bar and wait for your punishment. Do not drink, just sit there."

"I promise you Chief, I didn't know." It didn't even cross my mind he did. He may be stupid, but he's not suicidal. I've known this boy since he was born.

"Everyone's here Chief, so we can get started with church," Brain lets me know.

"This is going to be short, so we can get this damn clubhouse searched. Let's go." Giles goes before me and everyone else brings up the rear. "No need waiting at the bar. Never thought your first meeting would be like this." I am very disappointed in Giles and I want him to know it. We make our way into the meeting, everyone but Hambone is here. I see Sinner has Sas in the corner and she is eyeing me. I walk to the head of the table and bang the gavel. "Alright, I'm going to bring everyone up-to-date and then vote. Then these two can get out and we'll finish." I look around at everyone, some look puzzled and others just pissed. "A man was sent in here today to plant a box in our clubhouse. We will talk contents and about the man after these two are gone. Giles was on gate duty and Sas distracted him with a blowjob, so this man could get in." I glare at Sas, and she starts her mouth.

"I was just paying Giles back for fixing my car. I didn't know. I'm innocent. I don't know why I'm dragged in here, I wasn't on gate duty." I look at Sas.

"Did I say you could talk? Shut your face before I shut it." Sas hears the tone of my voice and she shuts it down. "Orrin told us he was sent here and was told there would be a distraction. How fucking stupid do you think we are?" That took the wind out of her and she's speechless. Sinner stands up.

"Can I question Giles?" I know Sinner will be harder on him than anyone else, so I nod. Sinner comes and stands right in front of Giles and slaps him in the back of his head. "What the hell were you doing boy? Some whore shouldn't be able to lead you around by your cock. Tell the truth now. If you lie, it won't go easy on you." I would not want to be in Sinner's shoes right now.

"I told Chief exactly like it happened. Sas' car stopped by the gate. She said it died and wouldn't restart. I popped the hood and the battery cable was loose and I tightened it. She wanted to thank me. I told her she could when I was relieved of gate duty, but she said she had to leave. She kept rubbing against me and I gave in. The club was full, and it was slow, so I thought it wouldn't matter and nothing could happen. I'm sorry and it will never happen again." Giles looks at his feet and I believe him, but he's not ready to be a BlackPath member.

"Boy do you realize you could have cost us this club? Stand by your actions and look me in the eye. Saying sorry is a sign of weakness. I've taught you better than that shit." Sinner goes back and sits down.

"Giles go outside and sit on the bench until we're done. We'll tell you then your fate, don't try leaving." I don't want him in here for the rest of this, but we will have to punish him.

"Sas do you still say you did nothing wrong or are you going to tell the truth?" ZMan pushes her in front of everyone. I hate dealing with women this way, but she should have weighed her options more carefully.

"I'll come clean. You pissed me off because of the talking down you gave me the other night and when I was approached with a chance to make a grand, it was a no-brainer to me. I know the BlackPath MC don't beat on women, so I took my chances. I'm sorry. I still have part of the money if you want it." She is right, we don't hit women, but she betrayed us. There will be consequences. All the men look about ready to beat the shit out of her, but that isn't who we are.

"Who was the money from?" She looks about ready to piss her pants, so I know she's going to spill all of it. "Before you say anything, if you lie all the club ol' ladies will take care of you. That includes Joy.

"Joy is no ol' lady. She's a club girl just like me." She's grasping at straws. Like Kelsey and Chelsea couldn't take care of her by themselves.

"That's why we hired her, to keep you club girls in line. Tell us now." My patience is gone.

"Fine. Duke gave me the money to get the guy in. He didn't say why, so I don't know. I did what I do best." She is whining now. "Please, it won't happen again. I have learned my lesson. Duke just scares me."

"Do you have a number for him?" I know exactly how to handle this. People that push drugs usually sample their products. It makes them paranoid and they don't think things completely through.

"Yes." She hands me her phone and I pull up the number.

"Brain get us a burner and call him. Put it on speaker so we can all hear." Brain brings one of the phones over. He dials, and we listen to it ring three times.

Duke: "Yeah."
Chief: "We have your friends."
Duke: "Who the hell is this?"
Chief: "Dumbass figure it out. I said we have your friends."
Duke: "I don't have fucking friends, Chief!"
Chief: "They both gave you up and your package was destroyed. Get the fuck out of my town. This is Black-Path territory and you don't belong here. You have declared war distributing that poison in our schools. We are coming for you and blood will spill. You are a walking corpse now. Taking a vote now. I vote war and to let the two talkers walk."
Driller: "Yes."
Tazer: "Yes."
Shield: "Yes."

It goes around the table and it's unanimous.

Chief: "Did you get that? River of blood coming your way."
Duke: "We can come to a working compromise."
Chief: "No we can't. No drugs in our town. We are turning these two loose and then we will be coming for you."

I nod at Brain and he disconnects the call. Sas is crying, but I feel nothing for her. All I feel is anger. I see red and want to destroy everything that is Possessed Blood Souls. I know I must control this before I do something stupid.

"Tazer, tomorrow when Callie and Blake head back to Colorado, you and Jeb escort them halfway. I will get Dra to send someone to meet them there. Loaded for bear when you go." I'll be glad when they are safe and away from here.

"ZMan, you and Driller will get this Orrin and Sas and take them to Sas' apartment and let them out." Driller nods his head.

"You can't do that. He'll kill us for talking. You have to protect us." She really doesn't understand, but she will.

"That's exactly what will happen." I nod to Driller. He knows to get her out of my sight. He takes her to the door and it opens. Killman and Cutter come in, followed by Blake. "Blake can you watch her while we finish?" He takes a hold of her arm and escorts her outside. We have one more issue to deal with before we start the search.

"Okay, one more vote and then we need to search this club. Giles." I look at Sinner and he looks very calm, not how I would handle it, but I know he loves his boy. "Giles did wrong. I think we should take his prospect position, but he can try again in a year." I know some will want him barred, but I think he can learn from this, still, it's not just my call.

"I vote we let him retry in a year." Tazer and Giles are friends, I knew he would be first to vote.

"I vote we don't." Cutter is a hard-ass and I figured his vote.

"I vote retry," Shield says.

The vote makes its way around the table and it's not unanimous, but he gets to retry, and I can see the relief in Sinner's eyes. Sinner stands up and looks around the table.

"I just want to thank each of you. I know this could have been bad and it would have been Giles fault. When he comes back next year I will make sure his ass is straight." We each nod. We don't blame Sinner. He's a good brother. Loyal as the next. Always steps up when he's needed. He just needs to make Giles understand he must be committed if he wants in the BlackPath's. He sits back down with a relieved look on his face.

"Next I want everyone to think on the possibility of letting Blake in. Not today, but soon. He disposed of the drugs that were found and that is a solid for us. In fact, he has some things he wants to say, but today is not the day. Let's turn this place upside down. We also owe Joy's sister Em a big thanks. She's the one who thought the guy was suspicious. I don't know how no one else saw him. Brain, I want you to look at the surveillance tapes. I want answers. Anything else?" I look around and no one has anything to say. "Sinner stay so I can tell Giles. Everyone else get to looking." Everyone but Sinner leaves and they send Giles in. As soon as he is in front of me I see he's worried. The severity of his actions has finally set in.

"Giles you are out for at least one year. Do not come back to prospect until you are sure you have the dedication for it. This could have gone a lot worse and if it hadn't been for the respect we have for your dad, it would have. When you're a member of the BlackPath MC lives depend on you every day. That package could have been a bomb. We could all be dead. Do you understand?" I never take my eyes off him and he doesn't look away.

"Yes, sir. I understand, and when I come back, I won't fuck up again. You have my word." I don't know about him, but I will give him a chance to try to redeem himself. One day.

"Get out of my sight for a while." Giles and Sinner walk out. I look at my watch and it's getting time to go home. I type out a text to Callie and then one to Devil. I tell him to go ahead and leave. I text Hambone and tell him to stay until I get there. It's going to be a long night. Then my mind goes to Em. I need to thank her and let her, and Joy go. I get up and make my way down the hall to the bunk rooms. I knock on the door and it isn't long before Joy has it open. I see Em standing behind her.

"It's okay to come out now. Everyone is searching to make sure he didn't leave anything else. We've had prospects searching for two hours and nothing. Joy can you make sure everything at the bar is okay? I want to talk to your sister." Em's eyes go wide.

"Oh, sure. Chief this is my sister Em, Em this is the President of the BlackPath MC, Chief. Now that's out of the way I'll go check the bar and storage room." Joy is out the door before Em can say anything or react. I notice right off, her eyes hit the floor and stay there.

"It's okay Em, I just wanted to say thank you for stopping Orrin." She glances up at me but just for a second. Something about this woman draws me to her. I know I just met her and it's crazy, but I want her. She isn't my typical type, at all. Usually I like them tall, long-legged, big tits and a round ass. Em is beautiful, but she's not tall, barely five foot I would say. Her tits are nice, not too large, and she is a little thing. She'll do good weighing one-ten. No, not my type, but I want her. At over six foot I stand over her by a foot.

"It's okay. Anyone would have done it. I was just trying to help. Can I go now? I mean, to help Joy. I wouldn't bail on trying to help." I make her nervous. I move closer to her, but she moves back.

"Tell me about yourself." I know I should be getting out of here, but I just want to know more about her.

"Not much to tell. I just moved here. I'm Joy's younger sister.

I'm a widow. Not much else." She still doesn't want to look at me. I move closer, she can't move anymore because the wall is there.

"Do I make you nervous? You look nervous." I know the answer, but I want to hear her say it.

"Yes, you make me nervous being this close. I'm kind of shy." Joy said that about her, but I think it's my body this close to hers that makes her nervous.

"Is that all it is, or are you attracted to me because I want to kiss you? Do you want me to kiss you? Because I'm telling you Em, I usually do what I want to." I'm standing so close I can see the pulse in her neck. Her heart is beating fast. My cock is so hard it's rubbing against my zipper. I reach out and touch her face. "Sweet Em."

"No. I don't want you to kiss me. I'm a mar..." She cuts off as she realizes what she almost said, and she has a sad look on her face. I lift her face to mine and without even thinking I touch my lips to hers, swiping my tongue to her lips, she opens for me. I don't go too fast or hard. I savor her tongue and her taste. I deepen the kiss, but gently. I pull her body to mine and she crawls up my body until her legs are wrapped around me. I want her. I want to make her mine and just as that thought goes through my head, I release her, so she can put her feet on the ground and I pull away. Her face is beet red and she is breathing hard, and if that damn thought hadn't gone through my head, I would have loved to fuck the hell out of her, but I won't do this.

"I shouldn't have done that. Em, I'm not a nice man. You deserve a nice man. I tell you now it won't happen again. I don't kiss softly, I devour. I don't make love, I fuck. I don't do relationships, girlfriends, or marriage. I use. When I'm done, I walk away and never look back. You deserve those things I can't and won't give, so stay away from me. If not, I will fuck you and then

I'll leave you." I barely get it out and Em's face looks like she's going to cry. I can't handle crying women.

"I didn't ask you to kiss me. I don't want anything to do with you. I just want out of this room and out of this clubhouse." I step back from her and she goes around me and she is out the door. Like I said, a long night. *What the hell just happened? Need to get this job done and forget what just happened. I'll be keeping my distance from that woman.*

CHAPTER NINE

HOLDING
OUT FOR
FOREVER
BLACKPATH MC BOOK THREE

Em...

I can't believe that asshole. He kissed me and then he said he shouldn't have. What the heck? It's not like I asked him to. It's the first time another man besides Michael has touched me that way. I don't know how it happened. I don't know why I didn't stop him. Michael has been gone for three years, but at times when I first wake up I can still feel him beside me. Sometimes in my dreams I can remember him holding me. Feel his lips on mine and feel the way he made me feel safe. I didn't wash his favorite hoody for a long time, so I could still have his smell around me, and still when I miss him so badly I ache, I will put it on. He was the love of my life and I still can't imagine being with another man.

Michael and I were together since I was fourteen and he was sixteen. He was my first in everything. When I was twelve, Brad Peterson grabbed and kissed me and I punched him in the stomach, and that had been my experience with the opposite sex. Michael was my first boyfriend, my first real kiss, my first date, and my only lover. We shared everything. We were married as soon as I graduated from high school. We thought we could

VERA QUINN

struggle through college together and we did. There were a lot of
nights of studying, eating the cheapest meals we could find, and
then making love most of the night. Surviving on a few hours of
sleep and living in a small cheap apartment. I would go back
there in a second. We were so in love. I still cry for the time and
man I lost.

Michael graduated and was offered an excellent job and he
jumped at it. After a few months we were able to move out of
the small apartment and into our first house. We leased it, but it
had a yard. I was happy to be able to plant some flowers. I was
able to cook some bad meals. I still haven't mastered that whole
cooking thing yet. Most people would have called the two-
bedroom small, but it was a mansion to us. I graduated with a
business degree a little early and things were great, but Michael
wanted to give me more. I didn't want more, but he said it was
for our future. He took a contracting job overseas. I wanted him
home with me, but he said he could make more there than he
could at home. I hated it, but he said he would do it for four
years and then he would get a job stateside and we could start a
family and buy our first home. I was to get a job and establish
myself here. His first job took him to Kuwait and he was there
for six months and then home for one. I relaxed a little, but
when he was sent to Afghanistan for his second job I was on pins
and needles the whole time he was gone. He had just gone back
from being home for a month and I got the call. My world fell
apart. I felt like my heart was ripped out of my chest. I guess it
was, and I buried it with my husband. Now I just survive.

Joy has done her best to drag me back to the living, but my heart
just isn't in it. Of course not, I lost it three years ago. Then Chief
kisses me and thinks I want him. He's wrong, because to want
another man would mean I have forgotten Michael. I will never
forget Michael. Just from the one kiss I feel guilty. I don't know
why I reacted the way I did or why I didn't stop him. Chief is a
nice-looking man. Okay, to be honest, he's sexy as hell, but not

66

my type at all. Okay, I don't have a type. I had Michael. Michael was like the guy-next-door type. He was the guy next door. He was clean-cut, he had muscles, but not overly developed. He didn't work out every day. He was five feet ten and he looked hot to me, but he wasn't model perfect. Just perfect to me. Chief, on the other hand, is over six foot and he has muscles like he works out every single day. His hair is longer, and he has day old stubble. I was tempted to touch it. His eyes are dark and enticing. He has bedroom eyes. His lips are soft. He is an alpha male all the way around and I am intimidated by him. Although there is a definite attraction.

I know it was wrong to kiss him back, but it was so much more. It has been so long since I have had human contact like that or any way, and it was from loneliness, but it can never happen again. He didn't like it, and I don't do one-night stands. I don't do anything. I can't get involved because I don't have a heart to let anyone into or to give away. I buried it with my husband. Now to avoid Chief at all costs. Distance. Arrogant asshole.

CHAPTER TEN

HOLDING OUT FOR *FOREVER*
BLACKPATH MC BOOK THREE

Kim...

I can't believe Chief just sent me away. It's like he dismissed me. Well, he has more shit coming his way. He thought Duke's little surprise was shocking, wait until he gets mine. Yes, I know who is messing with the BlackPath MC. Knew it was coming. Duke and I know each other well. Stone and Duke do business on the side and my dad knows nothing about it. Chief's tech guy will find the connection soon. He's smart for a BlackPath member.

I saw Chief making eyes with that Em girl. I think she's Joy's sister. She better stay out of my way. If not, she will find herself in big trouble she doesn't want. She barely speaks to anyone and she isn't even woman enough to look anyone in the eye. I hate mousy women.

I have had enough for one day. Watching everyone slobber all over Callie and that brat she's baking. Devil won't leave her side and Ma would do anything for her.

If I'd known what Duke was planning, I could have helped him, but he never thinks things through. He's trying to hide things from his club and his brother King. The road names tell it all. Same thing as my brothers, except Duke did get the president position, but if he doesn't watch himself he won't have it long. The Possessed Blood Souls don't like the drug deals Duke is bringing in. They want to get away from them, but Duke likes the drugs. Sometimes I think a little too much. Him and Stone both. Duke likes the money they bring in. I'll have to give him a call and see if he wants my assistance. I'll wash his back if he'll wash mine. If Em doesn't stay out of my way I may need someone to take care of her.

It won't be long before I know if my plan worked. Two more weeks, and then I'll know if I need to start over. I can't wait to get home and update Stone on Duke's shenanigans. He will be pleased. Now if I can just pull Devil away from Callie so we can get back to Oklahoma. I hate waiting as much as I hate these people. Well, most of them.

CHAPTER ELEVEN

HOLDING
OUT FOR
FOREVER

BLACKPATH MC BOOK THREE

C hief...

Well it's been four weeks since Callie left to go back to Colorado. It feels like yesterday, but then again, it feels like forever. She's safe and that's all that matters. Her and Dra were married last week, and she's happy. So happy. They went off to Vegas and I guess that's for the best. Dra is a good man and he loves Callie.

We have information on where The Possessed Blood Souls MC has been holed up. Brain found them, but they move every few days. So, they have safe houses located all over. Someone must be helping them. No way they were this established around us and no one knows about it. Before the drug issue we had never had a problem with them.

Brain also found a link to someone we do know that has blood ties to them. Duke was Kizzy's cousin. That's before she was dealt with by Sarge. Duke also has a brother, King, who is in the Possessed Blood Souls and is not happy with how Duke runs things. In fact, from what we hear, his whole club is not happy with the drugs. It makes me wonder, if Duke can be linked to

Kizzy, can he be linked to Stone? That keeps jumping into my thoughts. My gut tells me yes. It's too much to be a coincidence. I don't believe in coincidence and I trust my gut. So, I'm warned and will progress carefully. We are keeping an eye on Stone. Uncle Rye is helping me out with that since he's already in Oklahoma.

Another thing bothering me is if Stone is involved, then that means Kim is, too. I haven't heard from her. Nothing. Not that I care, but before she most definitely had an agenda and now nothing. It's like waiting for that other shoe to drop.

Tonight, I'm at the clubhouse and I'm meeting with King. It's a meeting so I can look into his eyes when he tells me he wants his brother out. It would be the easiest way. Not as much bloodshed. They'll be out of our town one way or another, but I would like it to be with the least amount of bloodshed possible. I don't like stepping on the wrong side of the law anymore, but if it's necessary to keep our town free of drugs, it needs to be done. Sometimes a man has to do what he has to do to keep the people he cares about safe.

I'm sitting in the corner nursing my beer. Thinking and trying to figure out how to handle King. That's when I see Em come through the back to the bar, helping Joy again. They are carrying boxes of alcohol to stock. I hear them talking back and forth and they are bringing a smile to my face. They remind me of how Tazer and Callie used to go back and forth.

"Why are you being so slow?" Em asks Joy.

"What do you mean slow? I'm going as fast as I can. Is your ass on fire to get out of here?" Joy is smiling, but the question is one I want to know the answer to.

"Yes, actually. Chief said for me to stay away from him and I fully intend to. So, get cracking." Em is right, she does need to stay away from me. Looking at her, I can still remember that kiss and

71

how she made me feel. I would love to fuck her. They can't see me from where they are very well, and it being darker in this corner they haven't noticed me.

"You know sometimes Em your dense." Em stops and looks at Joy and puts her hand on her hip. In other women it would look ridiculous, but on her it's cute.

"Well Joy, you're a few fries short of a happy meal and these days that's not easy." Joy looks shocked, but she wants to laugh.

"And if stupid could fly you'd be a jet," Joy delivers it with a straight face but Em doesn't seem amused.

"Well, if Chief is only interested in thighs, legs, and breasts he needs to go to KFC and invest in a value meal, so he'll get more bang for his buck." Okay, Em is getting a little upset. She looks ready to leave, but Joy is just having fun at Em's expense.

"Em are you hungry? You keep mentioning food. Maybe you should try a Snickers." With that Joy cracks up laughing. I watch Em and figure she's going to lose it on Joy, but she starts laughing, too. "That sounds so good." Joy stops laughing for a second and looks serious, "Hearing you laugh again. It has been so long Em." She goes over to her sister and gives her a hug. "Maybe you're on your way to being fixed." Now Em goes completely quiet.

"I won't ever be fixed. My heart was torn apart, but it is better. Spending time with you again has helped. I'm okay. I found a decent job. I put a deposit on an apartment. The people just have to move out. I'm doing okay. Don't worry, Joy. I don't need more duct tape." The last one came out with a smile.

Joy is looking at her puzzled. "What the hell would you need duct tape for?" I'm confused by that one too.

"Grandpa always said if you can't fix something with duct tape you're not using enough." Both women break out in smiles. That is the corniest joke I have ever heard.

"That he did. Duct tape, super glue, and baling wire was that man's answer to everything. Okay, that's about everything. You ready to go get that pizza before we go home? You need to eat to take your meds. I need to get back here and run the bar tonight. Prospects have other things to do." Joy grabs her purse and they turn and leave out the back door. They never even knew I was there. Em is so beautiful. I wish I could have that beauty in my life, but I know I am no good for her and I need to stay away. She took my warning to heart and that's good. I haven't been with a woman that I cared about since Cheryl. I know I just don't have what Em needs.

Driller comes in the front door with King and a huge mammoth of a man behind them. As they get closer I notice the name Kong on his cut. He is their SAA. He is built for the job, that's for sure. They both come over and they sit at the table with me.

"Chief, this is King, VP of the Possessed Blood Souls MC, and this is Kong, his SAA. Why you are sitting in the dark corner?" I stand and shake each of the men's hands.

"The quiet is nice for a change." I notice ZMan and Shield walk in. "Grab us some beers on your way." They go behind the bar and get us all a cold one and then join us. "You wanted a meet, so get to it. What do you want?"

"You like to get right to it. Good. It seems our problem has become your problem, too." I drink slowly and really look at this man. He's probably my age. He's rough looking. Haggard I would say. "My brother Duke is out of control. He's on the same drugs he's selling on your streets and he's going crazy. He is unpredictable and can't be trusted. He killed that whore Sas after he beat and raped her. That man Orrin, he was dragged

73

behind Duke's motorcycle. Neither deserved what they got. He needs to be neutralized. We need your help."

"Why would I help you? I don't know you. What I do know of the Possessed Blood Souls MC isn't good. You sell drugs to children and they end up dead. That pisses me the hell off. Not a good thing for someone who wants a favor. You're on our turf. Only thing I can say is get the hell out before we put you out. I know you have help, or you couldn't stay on the move." I stop so he can say something. I need to know why he's here.

"You're right on all counts. I'm here waving a damn white flag. We are a nomad MC now. We have no home and we're tired. We need a place to call home. There's a place outside of Sedalia. It's still inside your protection area but it's small. We would like to purchase it from you. If I can negotiate this purchase, the club will back me in a takeover and Duke will be out. Without backing, he can't do shit. We won't run drugs in your town. You have my word." King wants to take his brother out. That would help us, but I won't give up anything.

"King, we have been here for years and I will give you nothing. We fought and shed blood over what we have. There is, however, a piece of land about ten miles from there, not under our protection, that is for sale. I know the owner. It's me. I own it personally. So, convince me why I want to help you stab your brother in the back. Seems to me if you stab your brother in the back you're not too damn trustworthy." I see he wants to say something, but he's also trying to show control. Kong has no expression at all.

"I have tried with Duke. He won't listen to reason. He won't listen to anyone. That whore and Orrin isn't even the worse things he's done in the past six months. He knows the drugs are laced with shit that can kill you, and he doesn't care. He keeps the good shit for himself and keeps cutting the rest. He has a partner. One you are very familiar with. They also have some surprises in store for you." He doesn't want to give too much away, but King is desperate and if I can see it, so can Duke if he's paying attention. I'll try a bluff.

"I've known Duke is in bed with Stone since we found Orrin snooping around. I also know Stone's sister Kim is involved but haven't figured that angle yet." He's watching to see if I have any signs of lying, I know I don't show any. I feel it in my bones Stone and Kim are in it with him.

"You're a calculating man, Chief. Stone is in talks with Duke, but I've only seen Kim with him twice. Stone hates his old man, brother, and anything BlackPath MC. Your daughter, too. Did you know Kizzy, Stone's ol' lady was our cousin? Duke and she were tight. They both had their problems with drugs. When Kizzy disappeared, Duke lost it." Brain said Duke and Kizzy were related, but he didn't find out they were so close. Well, Sarge better watch his back.

"We knew she was blood to the two of you. Is that why he has it in for us? Because we weren't the ones put a bullet in her, even if I wanted to. Get to the bottom line King. You're wasting my time telling me things I already know." Another bluff, but I want to know it all.

"Kim has her own agenda. She wants you. I heard her tell Duke. She wants to take your attention away from your daughter. She really hates your daughter. She thinks she has an ace-in-the-hole though. I know Stone is using her to keep an eye on you, or he was, while she was here. Stone wants all of you dead. He loved Kizzy and he blames you all. He also wants his dad and Devil gone. He especially wants that child of Devil and your daughter's dead. I would be keeping an eye on them. He says Devil deserves nothing. The only reason he hasn't gone after your girl is because she saved his ma from that ex of Kim's. He genuinely loves his ma. He thinks his dad has her brainwashed." There's something that bothers me and then it comes to me.

"Who helped Stone shoot at my daughter? He hired someone, and it only makes sense for it to be Duke if they're working together." He shakes his head.

"That was Duke and the only two friends he has left. None of the rest of us would follow him. He was supposed to kill Callie that night. He had been following her off and on for two months. He got teenagers to do it, so you wouldn't get suspicious. He questioned them about her friends and hangouts. Things like that. The rest of us don't want war. All we want is a place to call home and to settle down for a little while." I go over everything in my head he's said. It rings true to me. He said something though and I don't know why it bothers me.

"What is Kim's ace-in-the-hole? No woman controls me." She has nothing to hold over me and she hasn't even called me again. I have a bad feeling.

"I don't know. That part she didn't share, or if she did, we weren't told." I look him in the eye and if I was a gambling man, I would go with he is telling the truth.

"So, what you're proposing is we allow you to stay. I sell you the piece of property I own. We call a truce. You'll out Duke and not sell drugs in our town. What about Stone?" King is shaking his head.

"We'll out Duke, but Stone is your problem. We stay out of your way, but we don't have the resources to go after him. The Feral Steel MC would not believe us anyway. Stone and Kim are your problem. If Stone comes after us, we'll deal with him, but anything else is not our problem. We just want some time to settle." I see he's serious and I think this will be a good move.

"Give me a couple days. Two max, and I will have your answer. I'll have the club vote on it and if they give it a yes, then I'll sell you the property. If it's no, then I won't. Thanks for the information and if we find anything out, you'll hear from us." That's all I can give him. I believe him, but the club will decide. We both get out of our chairs and shake hands. King and Kong leave.

ZMan is the first to talk. "Do you believe him? Do you think he'd really take his own blood out?"

"Yes, I do. I think the whole club would. Did you look at their eyes? Those men are worn down. If they don't take him out now, he will get them all killed. Sooner or later Steel will get his head out of his ass and he will see what Stone has been up to. I don't like Steel, but he's one hell of a fighter. He will do what he must do and then he'll deal with the fallout. It'll cost him Kat, but he'll deal with that when it happens. He's a club man all the way. He shot his own brother for the club, so I know he'll go through with it. Vote tomorrow. Be sure to let everyone know it's mandatory to be here. This affects the whole club, so everyone needs to vote. I'm out. I need to unwind, so I'm going for a ride." I get up and go straight for the door. These last few months have been long. I need a damn vacation. I don't even remember what that is hardly. My last vacation was when both Callie and Tazer had to have their tonsils out at the same time, and you can't really call that a vacation. I think after Callie has the baby I will head up to the cabin for a rest. Me a grandpa. Imagine that.

I get on my bike and I just ride. I'm trying to clear all the shit out of my head. The riding usually settles this restless feeling. I look around and I see where I've ridden to, and I see I'm close to Joy's apartment. I know she was supposed to work this evening at the club tending bar. I wonder if she's gone. Em is never far from my mind. I don't know why. I've tried my best to stay away from her, and apparently she is doing the same. I drive so I can see the parking lot and I don't see Joy's car. I look up at the second floor and there's a light on in the apartment. I know I shouldn't stop, but for some reason I can find no excuse not to. I'm not one to deny myself what I want, and I want Em for the night.

I have my bike parked and I am up the stairs and knocking before I have a chance to give it a second thought. I barely tap on the door, and as I turn to leave she opens the door. There she is standing in a tank top and shorts. I look her up and down and my dick goes steel hard. I push the door the rest of the way open and step in. I pull her up to me and I crush my lips down on hers and devour her mouth. She opens for me and our tongues tangle. A growl leaves me. I must have her now. She climbs up my body and grabs my hair and I kick the door shut and turn her so her back is against the wall while I grind into her body. "Where's your room?" If she doesn't answer I will take her against the wall. I grab her tit and rub her hard nipple. Holy shit, I feel a nipple ring through her shirt. She's not wearing a bra and I need to taste her tit in my mouth. She still hasn't answered my question, so I turn and head for the sofa.

"What are we doing? We can't." She tries arguing, but I know she wants me. That was not a kiss a woman gives to a man she doesn't want. I sit down with her on top of me. She doesn't get up. I pull her in and grind against her. I hear a moan escape her. I reach up and take her shirt off and my mouth claims her nipple. I tease the tip with my tongue. I play with the ring. She is moaning, and I need inside her, it drives me crazy with need. I need to make her mine. Now.

CHAPTER TWELVE

HOLDING
OUT FOR
FOREVER
BLACKPATH MC BOOK THREE

Em...

I hear the knock on the door. No one comes to visit this late at night so I'm thinking Joy must have forgotten something. The knock is light, so I'm thinking she has her hands full, so I just open it and there in all his gorgeous glory is Chief. After the little talk he gave me, I'm shocked to say the least. He's looking me up and down and I have to say it's making me feel wet. I haven't had this feeling in so long. Chief wants me. I may not have had much experience, but I know what a look of need is. He needs me and to be honest, I need to be needed. I need to be wanted. I miss this.

He pushes the door the rest of the way open and steps in. I want him closer and it isn't long until he moves in and crushes his lips to mine. Damn, he tastes good. He doesn't give me the light kiss like before, he consumes me with his mouth and tongue. I want more. He dominates my mouth and takes my breath away. I need to be closer and climb his lean muscular body. I grab his hair and run my hands through it. Damn I want this. Did he just growl? That is so hot. I feel my nipples pebble. It's been so damn long. I hear the door slam shut. My back hits the wall and he grinds against my body exactly where I need it. I want him, now. I need him. "Where's your room?" Chief asks and I'm trying to clear my head. I feel almost drunk on total need. I know we're moving, but I don't care. I need him closer.

"What are we doing? We can't." But I don't mean it. He can't stop. He sets us down on the couch and grinds into me. I swear if he does that much longer I will come. A moan escapes me. My shirt is up and gone and he takes my nipple into his mouth and is playing with it and I feel the stirring in me. I know I need to stop, but I can't. He moves to the next nipple and I grind down on his cock.

"You keep that up and this isn't going to last very long. You are so beautiful babe." He lays me back on the couch. He's kissing his way down and everywhere he touches is on fire.

"Please Chief, I need you." I need him inside me. I need him to fuck me, now.

"When we're together call me Cameron or Cam, not Chief." I'll call him anything he wants if he fucks me. I'm squirming with need. He puts his hands on my shorts and pulls them off in one pull. I'm trying to help. His mouth is on my clit and I am grinding down on him. I grab his hair and push his head into me. I'm grinding onto his tongue and I feel it. A stirring, and then heat working up my legs, I am so close. He flattens his tongue and glides over me and then he starts sucking and I come undone. I am panting and then hold my breath when I feel the spasms begin.

"Oh shit! Yes, Cam, oh God...please yes!" I grind harder and he sucks until the spasms are gone. I feel lifeless, but I want more. I finally open my eyes and Cam already has his clothes off and his cock is huge, hard and waiting. He makes his way up to my mouth and he takes it ravenously. Devouring me. I'm overcome with need again. I taste myself on his tongue and the thought has me grabbing his ass and trying to pull him closer. I don't want sweet or gentle. I want hard and raw fucking. It's what I need. With one sharp movement Cam has his cock lined up with my pussy and he impales me with one forceful thrust. At first it's a little uncomfortable, but once he's in me completely I am in heaven again, and I want him to move faster. I need more. He is moving all the way in and sliding against my walls and then back out until all that is still inside is the tip, then he thrusts, and it takes my breath away. I am pushing with him and the walls of my pussy are sucking him in. Trying to suck his cock all the way in. I'm being greedy, and I want more. I am absorbed in the passion that is shining in his eyes. I can't take my eyes off his. His need is storming in his eyes and it is beautiful. He reaches and lifts my ass off the sofa and slams in and it's almost my undoing, but he feels it.

"Not yet sweetness. This time we come together. You are so fucking tight. Your pussy is heaven." Cam is breathing so hard; I can barely understand him. He has sweat rolling down his face. I clamp down hard on his cock with my muscles and I'm rewarded with a growl. I move my pelvis up hard and we slam together. He tweaks my nipple and it gives a slight bit of pain and I feel it starting. "Damn babe, you are sucking my cock with your pussy. Oh shit!" He starts slamming into me at a pace that is shattering me. I can't wait.

"Oh shit, Cam, yes. I'm going to... Damn it, faster, don't stop!" That's all I can take; I am unwinding with an earth-shattering orgasm. Oh crap!

"Damn I feel it! So, fucking beautiful." Then Cam goes quiet, but I can see on his face as his eyes roll the minute he feels the ecstasy. He keeps pumping. We are both soaked with sweat and I feel the cum leaking down the crack of my ass. We didn't use a condom. Oh, shit.

"Don't look so stricken. I'm clean. I always use a condom, you just made me forget darlin'. We'll get you the morning-after-pill to be sure." *Not likely. Some people may think that is okay, but not me.* I've been on the pill since I was a teenager. *What have I done? How did I let this happen? I'm not a slut. I don't do one-night stands.* This is the first time since Michael that I have even been with someone. "Turn that overactive brain off. We're going to rest for a little while and then I am going to wake up and we are going to fuck again. Tonight, you are mine. Don't think, just feel. I will make you feel things you've only dreamed of. I want to do so many things to that hot, tight, sexy body of yours and tonight you're going to let me. Then in the morning I'll go. We'll see what happens." He's snuggling my body from behind me. He is spooning me the way Michael used to and it feels so good. What's done is done. I will just have to keep my distance from this very sexy, hot man. My body feels so deliciously used but I don't know if I like that or not. I still and I just remember thinking this feels so good.

I wake up and I'm alone. I feel the bed beside me and it's still warm. I can't believe I had sex with Cam last night, and early this morning. I don't even know why I thought he would be here when I woke up. He said he didn't do relationships, but I still thought he would say something. Goodbye, something. I think about last night and still can't believe it happened. I look around my room and I see the picture of Michael on my dresser, and I am filled with regret. I need a hot shower to wash Cam's smell away. I dishonored Michael's memory last night and I feel ashamed. *How could I?* Somehow, I will have to deal with the guilt. I'll really have to stay away from the club-house now. I just hope Joy can understand. We are just now rebuilding our sister relationship from being away from each other so long. She'll have to understand that I don't want to have to see the contempt in Cam's eyes. He's had me and now he won't want me around. I am so confused. I should just bury my head under my pillow and not get up, but I have a job to get to. I look at my clock and the alarm will be going off in ten minutes. I reach over and click it off. It's time to face this day. I get up and head to the shower. It doesn't take long. I wish I had time for a long hot bubble bath. My body is sore. I just finish blow drying my hair when I hear a tap on my door. I open the door and Joy is standing there with a cup of coffee. I love my sister.

"I thought you might need this. I saw Chief's bike in the parking lot when I came in late last night and I couldn't keep from hearing you two. When you decide to come out of your shell you do it in a big way. How was it?" I know my face is three shades of red right now. I must have no shame left. I hadn't even thought of Joy coming in. She must think I am a slut now. No, she knows me better.

"I'm so sorry, Joy. I should have made him leave. I don't know what come over me. I just wasn't thinking." *I hope she believes me. This is just something I don't do.*

"Don't be stupid. Damn, Em. You needed to start living again and you were thinking with your body. Are you okay, Em? You know Chief is not really your type of guy. I mean I hope you don't think it meant something. No, that came out wrong. I mean..." Joy is skirting around the truth and I know it; she knows it too. I cut her off.

"It's okay, Joy. I know what you mean. Chief told me he doesn't do relationships. I understand. I was acting like a slut last night and that's not me. I hope you understand I will have to avoid your clubhouse now. I just can't face him. It won't happen again, but I was thinking while I was in the shower maybe I will start dating. Slowly. That guy in accounting asked me out and maybe I'll give him a chance. I can't dishonor Michael. So, dating maybe." I hope she understands.

"Em, what you did last night, there was nothing wrong with it.

You are single now. Chief is single. You're consenting adults. You did use protection, right?" Oops. Joy is waiting for my answer.

"No, we didn't. He said he was clean and always uses condoms. Michael and I never used condoms. I've been on the pill since I was sixteen for my periods. I know I screwed up." *What was I thinking?*

"You can trust Chief, but you took a big chance. We're making you an appointment to be checked just in case, and I'm putting condoms in your purse. Use them. No ifs, ands, or buts. You'll get something Ajax can't take off and I love you too much for that. Eat something before you leave so you can take your antibiotics, or you'll never get rid of that sinus infection." Joy is concerned, and I know she's right, but it's just something I've never had to worry about.

"Okay, *Mom*. I'll call for an appointment, but there will be no more casual sex. No more sex at all until I'm in a relationship. I'll grab something on my way to work. We need to shop." I hope she knows I'm sincere about the sex thing.

"I'm not judging. I just don't want you taking chances. We can shop tonight if you're up to it. I'm off tonight." She's right. I'm old enough to know the consequences.

"Okay, Sis. Shopping tonight. I need to put some mascara on and I am out of here before I'm late. You understand about the club, right?" I don't want to hurt her feelings.

"For now." Joy is smiling, and I know that means she'll give me a week or so and then she wants it back to normal. She is so like our mom.

"I've got to get a move on. I'll see you tonight. Love you, Sis." She's out the door. Time to get this day started.

CHAPTER THIRTEEN

HOLDING OUT FOR *FOREVER*

BLACKPATH MC BOOK THREE

C hief...

In the last three months, things have settled down some. We voted on the Possessed Blood Souls MC and it was unanimous. I sold the property to them. Duke got wind of the takeover from King and disappeared. King is now the sitting president. The drug problem caused by them has disappeared from our town. They are outside our area, and they stay there. I know Duke will be back. I would bet Stone has him tucked away somewhere. We've heard nothing from Stone or Kim, and they have left Callie alone. I haven't even talked to Steel again. It's been quiet around the clubhouse.

I've stayed away from Em. She's always sneaking into my thoughts, but I haven't seen her. Joy has been acting hostile toward me, but I guess she doesn't like the fact I fucked her sister. If it keeps up, I'll have to remind her we are grown-ass adults and it's none of her business. I still don't know what I was thinking staying the whole night with Em. I never do that. I also forgot to use a condom. Last time I did that Tazer was created.

Callie came home yesterday. Blake escorted her. Dra is still having problems. He said if it doesn't calm down Callie and the baby may be staying longer, but he hasn't told her yet. Wouldn't want to be in his shoes when he does explain, then he must tell her what he's been keeping from her. The call last night upset her enough. She knows he's keeping something from her, but with her and Devil asking Dra and Fe to be godfathers, it soothed it some, but tonight's call has her worried again.

We still haven't told her everything going on in our club, either. We haven't even told her Shield was voted in. He wants to let Sarge and Stealth know himself. He lied to Callie last night and told her no. He wasn't wearing his cut, so she didn't see his patches. He better be on that phone today. He wants to be the one to tell them where his loyalties lie. It must be hard for him since one is his twin and the other his best friend, but we have no problems with them if Diamondback stays in line.

Blake called last week and said the feud was heating up in Colorado, and it was more serious than what Dra is letting on. I hope the Troubled Fathoms know what they're doing. Blake and I have worked our problems out, and he's thinking about quitting his day job and moving back to Texas. It would be good to have my old friend back, but it's nice to have someone I know close to Callie. I know Blake would die before he let harm come to my girl. He's decided to stay the rest of the week instead of doing a turn-around trip.

Diamondback has been quiet. I have planned with Micah and Maddie to surprise Callie at Christmas. It's eight months away but Deb, their aunt, said it would be better then. She wants them to get used to the idea of having more family. I will respect her wishes. We still haven't found the brother yet, but we're not giving up.

Last night and today my house has been full of happiness and laughter. I have to say I've missed it. I always thought when Callie and Ty left home I would be happy. Sarah, Hanna, and Fe, with all their excitement of Callie being home, have me smiling. Devil and Kat haven't even bothered me this time. Neither talk to me very much, but I don't expect them to. They are here for Callie. All this is going through my head as I am about to go to sleep when I hear Callie yell and I am out of my bed. I get dressed as fast as I can, but by the time I make it to her room she has already gone into the bathroom. "What the hell is going on?"

"Her water broke. She's rinsing off, so we can go to the hospital. I called the doctor, he said for her to come to the hospital, so she can be checked." Oh shit! Dra needs get his ass here. I dial Dra's number and get no answer, so I try Betsy, still no answer. Same thing with Hawser. Then the door opens.

"Are you sure your water broke? It's still early," Kat asks.

"Well, considering I'm still leaking a little, it's a safe assumption. I need my phone, so I can call my doctor, and then Dra." I'm trying to help her, but I feel like I'm just in the way.

"Doc said come to the hospital. I tried Dra and got no answer. I called his dad and Betsy. No answer." Devil got the same as me. I'm not liking this, but right now my baby needs to get to the hospital.

"Fe, get my hospital bag by the closet door and call Sarah and Hanna. Dad, can you get the SUV out front? Devil grab the bag in the kitchen to take, and Kat can you stay with me and make sure they don't run off and leave me? Uncle Blake, please, keep trying Dra. Can you bring your SUV, also? Kat, you may want to call Kim. I am going to try and call people on the way to the hospital. Let's move people." We may be a little unorganized, so Callie is taking over, but if it keeps her calm, then that's what needs to happen. We make it to the hospital in record time. Callie is on her phone the whole way there. She still can't reach Dra and she's worried—to be honest, so am I. Callie is dilated to a four and they have set her up in a birthing suite. She was resting, and she swears she saw Dra. The pain must have her delirious. She's stubborn and won't take any kind of pain medication. She's always been that way with pain meds. She thinks because her mom had an addiction, she might be more likely to get addicted. She won't listen to reason.

We have gotten word from Colorado. Blake finally reached Krill and there's been an explosion, and they don't think there are any survivors. We won't tell Callie anything. Dra could have been in there. In fact, he probably was. Now I need to call Devil out here and let him know. We've all been pacing the halls. She's going to know something is up, but she'll just have to wait. I push through the door and see my baby in pain, this is killing me.

"Can we speak to you out here for a minute?" Devil makes his way out to the hall. Shutting the door behind him, I make sure the door is shut. "It's bad." All the men that have been in Callie's life are here. Diamondback, Sarge, Stealth, Tazer, Shield, Blake, and Driller are all here, and there's nothing we can do to protect her from the physical pain she is enduring bringing her child into this world, or the mental pain she's going to feel afterwards when she must face the devastating news that's coming her way. I'm about to go in when the door opens and out walks Callie.

"Why the hell aren't you in that bed?" Devil is shocked she's up.

"Because some assholes think they can keep shit from me about my husband just because I'm in labor!" It's no more out of her mouth then she's bent over in pain. She is trying to do her breathing. "Mother sucking biscuits."

We can't help but laugh at her strange choice of words. She gives us a go-to-hell glare. Sarge moves over next to her and rubs his hand down her back. He still has it bad and seeing her this way must be killing him.

"Are you okay Callie?" The boy can't help himself from trying to help her. She takes his hand in hers.

"I'm okay Mase. Just hurts like the dickens." I think he would take her pain if he could.

"Tell me what is going on with Dra. I want to know now, or I won't go back in." I look at Devil, but we both know Callie has no control over what she's going to do right now. "What the hell is so funny?" Callie is throwing a hissy fit and it will do no good at all.

"Well Daughter, I understand you want to know about Dra, and we are looking into it, but you won't have a choice about going back in, because Baby Girl, that baby is coming. You can't change that." She can't change anything right now.

"Now get your ass back in that bed until our son is born. If I know Dra, he would be the first to tell you to do just that." Devil is losing his patience with Callie, but he needs to put in check. She's worried, but she turns and goes back into her room. I look Devil straight in the eye.

"Do not lose your temper with her. She is going through enough, and she has more to face. Now you get back in there with her and hold her hand and try to keep her mind on delivering my grandson. I'm going outside to try and make a call to Krill to see if he has found out anything more. My phone is getting shit service in here. I will be back in there in just a few minutes." Devil goes back in and Blake and I head for the elevators. Diamondback, Sarge, and Stealth can wait outside the door and keep watch.

As soon as the elevator doors open I'm out with Blake right behind me. As soon as I'm outside my phone rings, I look, and it's Krill. "Yeah."

"They're gone. All three were in the explosion, and they're all gone." Krill voice is full of anguish.

"Calm down. Did you see the bodies? Are you sure?" If there was an explosion, maybe there's a mistake.

"The only body they recovered was Gram's, but they were there. No survivors. We are at war and we're going to burn their shit down." Krill is losing it, but if I was in his shoes I would be in the same shape or worse. He needs to keep it together for his club.

"Listen to me Krill. Shut your mouth and listen. I understand you want revenge but keep your head. As soon as Callie has this baby, we'll be there to help. They will be expecting you. It will be a trap. Are you hearing me? I owe your family. Your club protected Callie when she first went to Colorado. I pay my debts. Dra is family. So, you are family. Let Kellan be born, and we will be there. We will take them out together. Just give me time. I give you my word. Now wait. Think of your damn club." I know it will be hard, but he just needs to wait. Callie's heart is going to be broken again. I know she's a strong woman, but everyone has their limits. She has been so happy. My mind goes to Em. *What I wouldn't do to see her right this minute. What the hell?* "Krill you still there? Just sit tight." I hang up; I hope like hell he listens. I look at Blake. He heard everything.

"Who the hell would hurt such a sweet lady? They need to die." This is not the Blake I have seen lately. Not in many years.

"What are you saying, lawman?" I see the anger in his eyes.

"Not anymore. I'm hanging my badge up as soon as this baby is born. When you go after them, I will be going, too. No badge." I have my best friend back completely. I slap his back.

"Let's get back to Callie. Fill everyone in but be sure everyone knows to keep it quiet until I tell Callie." We both head for the elevator. My mind is still on all the events when the doors open. The first thing I see is Stone. Then I see the group of people outside Callie's room.

"Chief, I was just coming to look for you. Callie wants you." I shake my head but say nothing. As I get closer to the door Kim steps out from behind Steel and her hand is running over her rounded belly. Kim is pregnant. Oh shit... I used a condom, surely it can't be mine, but she locks eyes with me and nods her head yes. I must know.

"Is that mine or are you whoring around with someone else?" I know I'm being an ass, but too much is happening too fast. "I used a condom every time. We didn't have unprotected sex."

"I did this on purpose. The condoms I gave you had tiny holes poked in them every time. Now you're tied to me, and I know you won't abandon your child, so we will be together." I look at Steel and he has a tough time looking at me. Kat won't even make eye contact.

"I had nothing to do with this, but she's my daughter, and this will be my grandchild, so I can't just disown her." Well, if that isn't just great. I can't deal with this right now. I start to go in the door and I hear Stone and I turn on him.

"Stone, why don't you tell Steel about your business with Duke. You know, Kizzy's cousin? The drug pusher to children. When I get back out here, you better be gone." Then I look at Kim. "When this child is born I want a DNA test, and until then I will help with medical bills only. Stay out of my way."

"You can't do that. I'm having your child. You must take care of me. I deserve to be taken care of, and you owe me," Kim says in a huff. I can't deal with this right now. I walk through the door and try to block it out for the task at hand. Time to meet my grandson and then time to break my daughter's heart.

CHAPTER FOURTEEN

HOLDING OUT FOR *FOREVER*
BLACKPATH MC BOOK THREE

Em...

It has been three months since I've seen Chief. As in, set eyes on him. He has successfully avoided me, and I him. I'm sitting here on the side of my bathtub looking at the home pregnancy test and it has a plus sign. I look at the next one and it has two lines, and the third is pink. All positive. *Well, hell. How did this happen? I mean, I know how it happened. What do I do now?* When Michael was alive I always dreamed of having his child. Then after his death I hated we had waited. It was smart. We didn't have a lot. We struggled and couldn't afford a child, but still I will always wonder what if. Now I'm carrying another man's child. It doesn't seem right.

First things first, I need to make a doctor appointment. These could be false positives. Then I think, I have been sick in the mornings some, but mostly late at night. More just a sick feeling, not actually throwing up much. My boobs have been sore. I look down at my stomach and it's still as flat as it usually is. A doctor's appointment today, if possible. I don't even want to think about having a conversation with Joy about it. She will lose it.

At least I won't see for her three more days. Today is Tuesday, and she always meets me on Fridays for lunch. I finally moved into my own apartment three weeks after the Chief incident. Joy has moved into the clubhouse, so I don't go to see her. She always makes it easy on me and meets me somewhere. Just as I am thinking this all over, my phone buzzes with a text.

Joy: Are U up?

Me: Yes. Getting ready 4 work.

Joy: Chief's daughter had her son.

Me: Good.

Joy: Want to go with to see?

Me: No

Joy: Thought I'd ask. Can't hide forever. See U Friday lunch?

Me: Yes. See U then.

Chief is a grandfather, and I may be pregnant with his child. Not good but I'll deal with it. Home pregnancy test aren't a hundred percent or I'm in denial.

I make it to work and today I feel off. Not sick, but sluggish. Not enough sleep. As soon as I have a minute, I make a call to my gynecologist and tell them what I need. The nice receptionist said if I just want a pregnancy test there's no appointment needed, I just need to run by on my lunch and do the test. She also warned that home pregnancy tests are reliable if done correctly. I'm not a nurse, I could have made mistakes. She said they would call me with the results if I set up a password. My boss doesn't like me having extra time off, so this is good. My morning goes fast. I keep busy and it's lunchtime before I know it. My stomach has settled so I'm ready for a grilled chicken salad. My favorite lunch. Doctor's office first. It only takes a few minutes for the test. They went ahead and drew blood just to make sure. I devoured my lunch and made it back to work right on time. I get caught up in paperwork and filing, so that it's four-thirty before I know it. I wouldn't have even have noticed, but my phone rings. I get to it before it stops and notice it's the doctor's office. Suddenly, I have butterflies in my stomach. This call could change my life. I answer and try to be very nice as she asks me my password. My mouth goes dry and I feel sick as she tells me my test is positive and I need to set up an appointment, so I can get on vitamins and have an initial exam. I barely remember getting off the phone or making my way home.

I'm sitting on my sofa trying to come to terms with the fact I am going to be a mom. *How can I be a mom? A very single mom. I must tell Chief. I have to tell Joy.* Then I hear someone at my door. Who would be here? I open the door still in shock. When I open the door, Joy walks in and she is jabbering away.

"You will not believe what that bitch did to Chief? She poked holes in the condoms, so she would get knocked up. What kind of woman does that?" *Wait what did Joy say?*

"What did you say? Someone else is pregnant by Chief, too?" I know when it comes out of my mouth Joy would pick up on it. I wasn't thinking.

"What the hell do you mean someone else?" Joy is gripping my arms and her voice sounds a pitch too high.

"What did you say first?" I need to know what she said.

"Kim got pregnant from Chief by poking holes in the condoms. Now tell me what you mean?" Joy lets go of me but is still upset.

"I've been feeling sick and haven't had my period. I took some home tests." That's all I get out.

"They could be wrong. You need a blood test." Like I didn't think of that.

"I had it today at the doctor. I'm pregnant." I know she's disappointed in me and I'm sorry for that.

"Oh, crap." Joy sits down heavily on my sofa.

"Understatement of the year." Don't I know it.

"I'm going to be an aunt. How cool." Joy is smiling.

"What do you mean cool? Nothing cool about it. I'm going to be a single mom. I got Chief's message loud and clear and now some other woman is having his child, too. So not cool." Joy has lost it.

"Chief will take care of his child. He's a stand-up guy that way. You are keeping it?" *Has she lost her mind?*

"Of course, I'm keeping it. I just don't know if I'm staying here. I will tell Chief, but I think he may have his plate full. I need to relocate. In fact, I'm going to go tell him tonight and then I'm going to weigh my options." Some distance may do us all some good.

"I won't be there to help you. Please don't. I'll go with you to tell Chief, and then you can think about it." I knew she wouldn't like the idea, but I need to consider everything. Chief was sure he wanted no kind of relationship, and now with another woman pregnant by him, I need to tell him tonight before I lose my courage.

"Okay. Let's go and I'll tell him. Will he be at home or the clubhouse? I need to do this before I lose my courage. I have plenty of time to make up my mind. Besides, you could go with me." I know I can't ask her to up and leave her life.

"Chief will change your mind. I know he will." Joy is very convincing.

CHAPTER FIFTEEN

HOLDING
OUT FOR
FOREVER
BLACKPATH MC BOOK THREE

C hief...

I just had to tell my daughter the man she loves is dead. She has had such turmoil in her short life. Devil thinks he's getting her back, but he will back off and give her some room to breathe. Callie has Kellan to hang onto now. Tomorrow I will make plans to avenge Dra's death. I owe the Draven family that. I owe Callie that. I down another shot and I hear a noise behind me. There she is, the woman I despise. She got herself pregnant to trap me. What she doesn't know is I will never be trapped. I will take care of my child, but she means shit to me. In fact, I can't stand to look at her. "What are you doing in my clubhouse? You have no reason to be here. I told you I want a DNA test, and I will pay for doctor care, and no more. End of story."

"You don't mean that, Chief. We can be good together. You won't let me take your child away from you, and if you don't take care of me, then that is exactly what I will do. The brat means nothing to me but a means to get you. You want it, then you take me. We are a package deal." She is crazy.

"Kim do not threaten me. I will take your ass to court. I will sue you for full custody." I will also put her to ground if she hurts my child.

"I will disappear. Can you live knowing you have a child out there you can't protect? I think not." She hasn't investigated my divorce very closely. "Where is everyone? This place looks dead."

"None of your damn business." She doesn't need to know everyone is getting ready to ride to Colorado. Then I hear the front door and in walks the woman who has been starring in all my dreams for the last three months. No, she doesn't need to be around this bitch. I see Joy behind Em.

"Joy take your sister out of here. This is a private conversation." Em doesn't stop and neither does Joy.

"Do you want me to put this piece of trash out of here?" Joy is very protective of the club and I could see her hauling Kim out of here. If Kim wasn't pregnant I would enjoy it, too.

"I said private conversation, Joy." She needs to get Em out of here.

"I'm right here. Can't you talk to me? I have something I need to tell you. I went to the doctor today and there's something you need to know." I see Em is determined to tell me something.

"Listen bitch, did you not hear him? We are having a private conversation and you two need to leave now before I have him put you out." Kim is getting on my last nerve and I'm going to go off on her if she attacks Em.

"Chief, I'm pregnant. I'm having your baby." Kim goes towards Em, but Joy steps in her way. I did not just hear what I thought I did. She's carrying my baby. Two pregnant women. I don't want any more babies. I told her to stay away from me. *Why can't anyone listen to me?* I told Dra to be careful. I told him to call us for help. I told Kim I didn't want her, and I told Em to stay away.

"I told you to keep your ass away from me. I don't want any more children. Not from you and not from her," I point at Kim. "So, take your ass away from me. How do I even know it's mine?" All the hate I have inside me is coming out at Em. I want to hurt someone, and she's the one in front of me. I see the hurt in her eyes. Her hand goes to her stomach protectively. Then I see the pain I have caused. She does as I knew she would. She turns and runs out. Tears running down her face.

"I never thought I would say this, Chief. I have always respected you, but you are a bastard. She was just trying to let you know. Unlike this bitch, she wants nothing from you. She knows she'll be a single mom, but you can damn well bet she won't be alone. I quit." Then Joy turns and leaves, and I'm left with the woman I can't stand instead of the woman I can't get off my mind. I watched as the only woman I have cared about since my son was a baby walks out of my life without a fight.

"That child is probably not yours anyway. Our child is most definitely yours. She's just another bitch looking for a meal ticket for her bastard child." That's it.

"Listen bitch, get the hell out of my clubhouse and I don't want to see your ass again until we can have a DNA test done. Go and don't come back." All I feel for Kim is pity.

"You'll want me back and then I will make you beg. Your darling Callie is going to find out exactly what kind of man you are." This woman really doesn't know or understand Callie at all.

"What you don't understand Kim is we know exactly how jealous of Callie you are. We know you set Kat up to be shot by Deacon. We know Stone is setting Steel and Devil up to be taken out. We know that you two have been stealing from Feral Steel MC. Now let me see, should I come up with the hard proof and hand that over to Feral Steel MC? How do you think they would react? Let's not forget about Duke and Stone having shot at my daughter. You can either go to Stone with it and you two can try to run, but just so you know, Steel is the one who put his brother in the ground for betraying the club. What do you think he'll do to you and Stone? You're going to go home and when this baby is born we will have a DNA test done. If this child is mine, it will be raised by me. One way or another. You've got, what, four months or so left? You better choose wisely, or you will find yourself on the wrong end of someone's club." I say it with as much maliciousness as I can. I hate this woman. She looks scared and torn on what to do. "Leave now, Kim." She gets up without a word and leaves.

I now have two women pregnant. One I trust. One I have more feelings for than I have in a very long time. I destroyed her tonight, without thinking. I just let the hate for Kim roll out onto her. Then there's Kim. A woman I detest. She would stab me in the back without a second thought. Her insecurities make her poison, and her I let walk out of here. I rub my hand down my face. Right now, I am no good for Em. I need to go take care of the job I have taken on and then I'll come back and try to put my damn life back together. After that, I'm taking a fucking vacation.

CHAPTER SIXTEEN

HOLDING
OUT FOR
FOREVER
BLACKPATH MC BOOK THREE

Em...

I came home after the awful confrontation with Chief and cried myself to sleep. I sunk into the pits of hell with self-pity. It will be the last time. I can do this on my own. I heard Joy come in early sometime this morning. She must have used her key to get in. She must have known I needed time to myself because she didn't come in to check on me. She is the best sister I could ask for.

I got up and took care of brushing my teeth and peeing for the third time. I don't want to face Joy, or anyone, but I will. I just need to get a plan formed first. I can understand Chief wanting nothing to do with me, but not to want his child, I don't understand. In fact, it pisses me off. I know I can't stay here. I don't know where to go, except back home. It makes sense. I have some friends there. I already have a doctor I'm comfortable with there. If I ever need help, I will have people I could ask. I know I can get my job back, because they begged me to stay and as of last week they haven't replaced me. Mrs. Langston calls every week and checks in with me. If Chief ever comes to his senses, he can make the drive to see our child. It's not across the country, just a little over a hundred miles. Enough distance to be comfortable. Joy can come visit when she can. I will miss her. We have become close again. Closer than we've ever been. I reach across my bed to my nightstand for my phone and send Mrs. Langston a text, and then I send another one to my office telling them I won't be in today. I need the time to get everything lined up. I no sooner put my phone down when I get a text. Mrs. Langston responded, and I can have my job back. She's looking forward to having me home. I text her back and tell her I need to give notice and then I'll be there. First hurdle done.

I get up and grab my laptop off my dresser and try to form a plan. I look at real estate firms in Pittsburg and Mt. Pleasant. Either will work. Even Gilmer would work. Pittsburg is in the middle. I want to lease, so I contact Jennifer. I know she handles leases and sales in the biggest real estate company in Pittsburg. We went to college together. I send her an email with my requirements and hopefully she can find me something. I still have money put back from Michael's insurance I haven't touched. I'm not a big spender, and I knew I might have a rainy day. Well, it's storming outside right now. I also send a text to the apartment manager where I'm living. I will need to find out what it will take to get out of my lease. Now all I have left to do is tell Joy. I dread that, but she'll understand, surely. For some reason, now that I have formed a plan, I feel calm and it feels right. This may not be the ideal time to be pregnant. This may not be the ideal situation. Chief isn't the ideal man to be the father, but I will love this child more than anything in this world. Joy will love my child. Calm. I am calm. I can do this. I look at my clock and it's close to eight. No time like the present to face Joy. I know she's up. I heard her moving around. She must really be worried. She's not usually an early riser. I may as well take the bull by the horns as my grandpa would say. I take my phone and laptop and go into the kitchen where my sister is sitting at the table. She looks rough. I can imagine after crying myself to sleep last night I look about the same. I didn't even bother to look at a mirror.

"Hey Sis. You want me to fix you some breakfast?" Joy doesn't cook and neither do I, so I laugh. "What? I can manage toast." She laughs with me and I know it'll be okay, but I am going to miss her.

"I've come up with a plan. I'm going back to Pittsburg." I try to rush through, so she doesn't interrupt me. "I'm going to miss you, but I can't stay here. I want and love this child already, and I know it's not ideal, but it's a fact, so I want to enjoy it all. But, I can't do that with Chief telling me he doesn't want this child. I understand he doesn't want a relationship. I didn't do this on purpose. He was there that night too, and he could have worn a condom. He came to me, not me chasing him. I can't believe he doesn't want anything to do with his child, but I would never stop him from being in his or her life. I think I'm happy for the first time since I lost Michael." I got it all out. It was jumbled but I hope she understands.

"Stop. I know. I'm going with you. I know Chief has a lot on his plate right now, but that was no reason for him to go off on you. You're not Kim. You didn't plan this, but I think he was so shocked you got lumped in with her. Doesn't matter. He treated you horribly. I never thought I would lose my respect for Chief, but the man he was last night I do not respect." I can't let Joy give up her life here for us.

"Joy, you can't give up your life here for us. You love it here. Just ignore this and go back to work." Joy comes around the table and takes my hand, then she's leading me into the living room. As soon as we enter, I see her stuff stacked in the corner. "It's done. I quit. I moved. I just hope I have a place with you and my niece or nephew." I don't know what to say.

"Of course, you have a place with us. I want you with us. I just didn't want to be selfish and ask." We hug each other, and I know this is the right thing to do. "I'm getting my job back and I've contacted Jennifer to find us a place, but I need to add a bedroom. I sent an email to find out what I need to do to get out of my lease. I need to call and talk to my supervisor. I called in sick today."

"You've done all this and it's not even nine yet. Wow. So how about feeding your baby?" I just hope Joy will be okay with Pittsburg. It's a whole different kind of town. It has one grocery store, some auto-parts stores, a few restaurants, and fast-food places, and convenience stores. We must go to the next town to go shopping for anything else. It's small-town living. They roll the streets up at five, but it's quiet, and everyone knows everyone. In the good, and bad ways. Gossip galore, but everyone says thank you and please, and men still hold the doors for their wives. I didn't know I missed it so badly.

"Not yet. Maybe around ten. Right now, my stomach is unsettled." I set my laptop up on the table and send Jennifer another text about needing a three bedroom and not a two. I write a resignation and in it I only let them know I'm pregnant and moving. I send it off. Two weeks is the standard, and that's what I give. I think about what else I need to do while Joy goes about making coffee. It smells so good, but I need to limit my caffeine intake. My mind goes back to the one night that has changed my life. I can almost feel Chief's lips on mine. His arms lifting me, but my computer dings and brings me out of my haze of memories. It's from my boss's office. I open it and it seems since I called in today and I'm still on my probationary period I'm no longer needed, so my resignation is accepted immediately. So much for being courteous. Just as well. "Seems as long as I can get out of my lease we can leave soon. My resignation has been accepted and no notice necessary. Good thing I don't need a reference."

"Let me talk to your apartment manager. I know someone looking for an apartment in a better area; you can get out of it if you have someone ready to lease. I'll go to the office now since you already texted them and talk to her." Joy is amazing.

"Are you sure? I'll take care of it if they don't agree. I have the money to pay the lease off. I just don't want to spend the money if I don't have to. That's the reason I saved from my job to get this place. Once I put money in savings I hate to take it out. I guess Michael and I barely getting by for so long taught me to save as much as possible. I still have his life insurance in the bank. I haven't touched it since I put it there. I paid what I had to and then put the rest in savings and left it there." To tell the truth it feels like tainted money.

"Michael was smart to get insurance. He was always thinking of you. You two loved each other so much. I hope one day someone will love me like that, and I hope you find it again." I don't think it's in the cards for me. *Don't you only get one great love in your life?* I've had mine, but I hope Joy gets it. She deserves it.

"You will find it Joy or it will find you. Michael was it for me. I have bad judgement in men now, or I was just lonely. I am so attracted to Chief. Something about him draws me to him. I think now I need to concentrate on my child-to-be." I wish it could be different. I think of Chief all the time. It catches me off guard at times. He's in my dreams, and my daydreams. I need to stop this.

"You said you're attracted to Chief. As in present tense. You care about Chief, don't you? It wasn't just a one-night stand for you." Oh crap. I didn't mean to let that out to Joy. Now she's going to worry.

"Doesn't matter. He isn't interested. He's made that clear." Very clear, very loudly.

"Okay, Em. You're right, we need to leave as soon as possible.

The last thing you need in your life is a crazy-ass biker. I am going to go talk to the apartment manager." Joy is up and out the door. I have decided to donate my furniture. All but the bed was secondhand anyway. I'll get more when we get there. Between our two vehicles we can get everything there. I hear a ding on my computer and it's Jennifer, she has three places available. I let her know I'll be in touch with her this afternoon. Everything is falling into place. I have shut my computer down and gotten up to find something light for breakfast when I hear Joy come back in.

"If we can be out of here in two days and there's no damage, all you'll lose is the last month's rent you put up and the security deposit. That's a good deal. She has a couple wanting an apartment, but it has to be fast." I text Jennifer and let her know we'll be there the day after tomorrow.

"Are you sure you want to go and leave your life here Joy? I hate for you to give it up because of me, but I'm going. As soon as I have everything packed, then I'm gone. I did everything I could to let Chief know, so I have nothing to regret." I want her with me, but I would never expect it.

"Already done sweetie. We are all we have, so let's get cracking and get us on the road to our new lives." Joy's right.

"Okay. Let's do it." I am excited for the first time in a long time.

CHAPTER SEVENTEEN

HOLDING
OUT FOR
FOREVER
BLACKPATH MC BOOK THREE

K im...

Chief threw me out like a piece of garbage last night. He will come crawling back. That other bitch is not getting in my way. If she tries, it will be her biggest mistake. Chief is mine, he just doesn't know it yet, but he will. I will use this child to lure him in. He may be busy now, but when he thinks about it, he will want me. I know the kind of man he is. He's all about family. I'll give him his DNA test, and then I will take him to the cleaners and get everything I want. When I'm through with him, he'll wish he never met me.

He rattled me last night. I can't believe he knew about mine and Keifer's embezzling from the club. Technically it's Keifer, he's the treasurer. I was also shocked he knew about our connection with Duke. I can't warn Keifer though, because he might run, and I need him. Chief won't tell Dad or Devil right now, so we're still safe. Chief was wrong though, no way did Dad shoot his own brother. He loves his family and would never do such a thing. Some men put the club first, but Dad would protect us. Wouldn't he? Now I'm not sure. No matter. Chief is too busy to let him know. That means I have time to get on Chief's good side and then he'll protect me, and I won't have to worry about it. If all else fails, I can go to Duke. He wants me and would never let anything happen to me. I have options. Keifer on the other hand is just fucked if he gets caught.

I'll just be glad to spit this child out. My hips are getting wider and I'm getting stretch marks. One good thing, the girls are larger, and I play them up. First thing on my list is a nanny. I won't be breastfeeding, so the nanny can take care of the child while I do what I want. I need to stay one step ahead of Chief and my dad. I'm not going back to Oklahoma for a few days. That way Mom has time to worry, and when I get there, she'll let me have whatever I want. I'll play the dutiful daughter to be able to keep close tabs on what's going on. That brat of Devil's is not getting what is mine. If all else fails, once this child is here I will be able to get whatever I want from my parents just to keep me around with the child. I don't think I was meant to be a mom. I have no feelings towards the child at all. I don't care if it's a boy or a girl. I don't want to come up with a name. I guess I'll come up with some name with a K. Like Mom and Dad, to hook them even further. My next doctor visit I will have that sonogram thing. Mom is going if I can't wrangle Chief into it; in fact, it will be the best time to get him to go. Perfect excuse. Once he sees the child, he'll be hooked. Perfect plan, I am one smart cookie. I remember how everyone was about Callie when she had hers done. The whole damn office was full of people who wanted to see. It'll be the same for me. Just three more weeks and we'll see if it's a son or a daughter for Chief.

Not going home yet. Callie has her many male admirers chasing after her at her dead husband's funeral. The brat is tucked away at Ma and Dad's. Ma said I could practice holding a baby while he was there. *I don't want to hold my own when it gets here, why would I want to hold a woman's who I can't stand the sight of?* I'll just look Duke up for some fun.

107

CHAPTER EIGHTEEN

HOLDING OUT FOR *FOREVER*
BLACKPATH MC BOOK THREE

C hief...

It's been four weeks since we rode into Colorado and burned everything the marijuana growers owned to the ground. Callie was able to get her vengeance, and I paid my debt, while keeping my promise to Krill.

Callie was strong as usual. She amazes me more every time she's tested in life. She rises above and survives. She's living with Devil and Kellan in Oklahoma. She said it's what Dra wanted, and I know it's what Dra told her, and he made Devil promise to take care of her, but I wonder if it's more. They are living in the same house together, but they're not a couple again, yet, but I have a feeling it's just a matter of time. Devil has never stopped loving Callie and I know she has feelings for him. Things work out in the strangest ways. Kellan is the spitting image of his dad, but I have seen Callie's stubbornness in him. He's the sweetest child. I love being a grandpa.

My mind turns to Kim and my impending fatherhood again. She postponed her doctor's appointment a week, so I can go. She wants me there to find out if it's a boy or a girl. I need to go, but

I have no will to. I don't want to get invested until I have a DNA test, but I'm going. I will get to see Kellan and Callie while I'm in Oklahoma.

Rye and Bourbon have been keeping me updated on Stone's comings and goings. They would never let anything happen to Callie while she's there. She is, and always will be, their little princess, even if she is a grown woman. They have also let me know Duke has been around and him and Kim are still hooking up. They have some pictures just for Steel and Devil's eyes when the time comes.

Then I think of my other child on the way, Em's child. Our child. I know that child is mine. I was a complete ass to her that night, and I have thought about going and finding her and apologizing, but I must deal with Kim first. I need to apologize to Em and Joy. I want Joy back at the club running the club girls and taking care of the bar. Things ran so smooth when she was here. I thought she would be back by now. I haven't seen her around town anywhere working, so she must be running low on money by now with no job. Surely if she had a job in town I would have run into her. I know what I want to do. I want to make Em mine. I have tried to get her out of my head, but I can't. I haven't even been with a woman since that night, and it has been months—four to be exact. Not my normal. First, I need to deal with Kim though. She is nothing but poison. I would never be with her; we would only poison the child with our hate.

I see Tazer and Shield come in the back door. Blake and ZMan are at the bar. Most of the members are here already. Today we vote on Blake, officially. He's been riding with us so it's time for a vote. He retired his badge and it's time we either give him his cut or cut him loose. He rode with us in Colorado like the brother he is. My faith in him has been restored and I think everyone else's has, as well. He apologized to Rye and Bourbon in person, and they accepted it. Today is his day.

I am about ready to head into my office when Driller and Hammer approach me. Driller looks like shit. I wonder what's wrong. Then I look at Hammer and he looks nervous. "What's wrong with you two? Driller you look like you slept in your clothes last night, and Hammer you look like you could jump out of your skin. What the hell is up this time?" Driller's eyes are bloodshot, so I know something is up with Laura. In fact, I haven't seen her around much lately and I'm an ass for not asking why.

"Can we go into your office?" Driller is barely holding it together, and I know something has happened to their baby. Not again.

"Sure Brother." I walk ahead of him, but I stop at the bar and grab a bottle of whiskey and three glasses. Then I walk into my office behind them, shut the door, and go and sit behind my desk. I pour each of us a glass and I wait to see who's going first. "I'm ready when one of you are."

"Laurie lost the baby last night, and this time they had to do a hysterectomy. I need some time off to help her adjust. I just don't know if she can come back from this. Kelsey is at the hospital with her. They had to sedate her." Driller has tears in his eyes. I know how much they wanted this child. This is the third time she's miscarried and the grief they feel each time is disheartening. I just wish there was something I could do.

"Why didn't you call me? I would have been there for you. It's what we do." I feel so bad for wallowing in the mess that is my life while my brother has been dealing with life and death circumstances.

"Laurie didn't want to contact anyone this time. She said she needed her privacy. She knew before we went to the hospital what was happening, and it tore her apart. She called her mom and sister. She says she feels like less of a woman because she can't even carry a child and she doesn't want everyone's pity.

Then when they had to do the surgery, she lost it. They've kept her asleep. I came to let you know I'll be away for a while. Kelsey is there until I get back, but I can't stay gone long, so right after the vote, I'll be gone until she can adjust." Driller is a private man, but I know this is killing him. Laurie is his life and they have wanted a child since they were first married.

"Brother, whatever you and Laurie need. Anything, anytime. You take your time. If there's anything you need to be brought up to date on, then I'll let you know." Here I am not wanting children with two on the way, and these two want children so badly.

"Thank you." That's all Driller can get out. He sits back and drinks his drink. I look at Hammer.

"I'm here to ask if someone else can be voted in as treasurer. I'm thinking Tazer would be good at it. He's good with numbers and he already knows our system from helping me. I still want to be a member, but I want to step back and have some more time off. I'm not a spring chicken anymore, and I think it's time some young blood has a chance." Then his eyes hit the floor. "I'm not as quick minded anymore. I think it best if someone else keeps an eye on the club's money." I look at him and I see he's embarrassed about saying this. He must be getting close to sixty. He's done his service to the club. He came to us late in his life, but he has always been a damn good brother. I know he's doing what he thinks is right or he wouldn't do it.

"Okay Brother, if that's what you want. No one is complaining though. The job is yours as long as you want it." He smiles at me and I know he's tired. I wonder if I'll have the courage to do what he just did when I'm too tired to do my job. He gets up and shakes both mine and Driller's hands and leaves. The weight of the world has been lifted off his shoulders.

Then I look at Driller and he has tears running down his face. I'm looking at a broken man. "Man is there something I can do?"

He's sitting there with his head in his hands. I walk around and sit in the chair beside him, then reach over and put my hand on his back. I have never been in his shoes, but I know what terrific parents they would be.

"I was so convinced this would be the time. She carried it longer than she did the others. I'm just empty inside. I was trying to be strong for Laurie, but I am full of so much grief. I will never be a father and she will never be a mother. We just always thought it would happen in time and there's no chance now. I don't know what else to say to Laurie to help her if I don't understand it myself." Driller is worse off than I thought.

"I don't know what to say. I have never been in your position. All I can think of is to be there for her. Have patience. Love her and listen to her. Not just what she says but pay attention to her actions. Get her some help with her grief, and remember you may need some, too. We're here for you. Whatever you need. We love you both, Brother." That's all I know to say. Now I'll just wait for him.

"Thank you, Brother. I just needed to let that out. I couldn't let Laurie see me that way. I know I have to share my grief with her, but she doesn't need to see the raw version right now." Driller will always protect Laurie from his inner demons.

"Are you ready for the vote?" I know Driller wants Blake in as bad as I do.

"Yes, I am, but then I have to get back to the hospital." Just like it should be.

"We'll send flowers tomorrow, but you let us know when she's ready to see us. Don't wait long, because we aren't letting you two go through this alone." I just want him to know we're here.

"Send a plant. She'll like it better." That we can do.

"You got it." We get up and head to our vote. We barely make it to the bar when I hear yelling. That sounds like Sarah. What the hell is she doing at the club? Then I know. Her and Tazer are at it again.

"Your damn name is Tyler David Black. There is no Tazer on your birth certificate. Why would you rather have some club girl give you a blowjob than to be with me? You had no problem popping my cherry when I was sixteen, and now you won't even answer my calls." Sarah is fit to be tied. Why Tazer doesn't just cut her loose is beyond me. I love the girl like she's my own, but she is a handful. I nod my head at Tazer and he knows to take it down a notch and handle her.

"Sarah, leave. I didn't ask you here, and we aren't together now, so who sucks my cock is none of your business. Next time knock. You don't belong here anymore. Leave, you're being a bitch!" Tazer is only making it worse.

"Do you mean that? You just called me a bitch. Do you really want me gone? I thought I meant something to you." Sarah is on the verge of tears, but I can't interfere.

"I've had you and I don't want you anymore. You're too high maintenance. I'm with club girls because I get mine, and then I don't have to put up with their mouths or the shit they do. You're still a little spoiled rich girl. I need a woman. Now leave. I don't want to see you again. We are done for good." Tazer is being cruel to her. Then right before our eyes Sarah changes. She stiffens her back and lifts her head and looks straight at Tazer.

"Okay. I get it. You'll never have to worry about seeing me again. None of you will." Then she looks at me. I'm sorry she's hurt, but until her and Tazer both grow up, they need to stay away from each other. She walks out without another word. Killman goes over to Tazer and they put their heads together. I walk up behind them.

"Do you think she fell for it? Do you think she'll go?" Killman is asking Tazer.

"What's going on? What's Killman talking about?" Tazer looks pissed.

"Sarah's parents want her to go back to school. This time in New York. She told Felix she wouldn't go because of me. I care about Sarah, and I can't hold her back from her education, so I set it up, so she would see me with Lita. That way she would be mad enough to go." So Tazer was trying to do it for Sarah's own good. Wrong method for a good reason. Sarah does need her education.

"That's what that was all about? Are you sure you can deal with the consequences when it backfires on you?" My knucklehead son is trying to be nice in a bad way. Sarah's not the only one that needs to grow up some. "Let's get to church, we have a vote or two to take care of."

CHAPTER NINETEEN

HOLDING
OUT FOR
FOREVER
BLACKPATH MC BOOK THREE

C hief...

We took care of what had to be done. Blake is now a BlackPath MC member. He doesn't have to prospect. He and Shield are now voted in as enforcers to help ZMan with SAA duties. Tazer is taking over the treasurer position from Hammer. Hammer is happier now as just a member. He was too worried about letting us down. Blake apologized in front of all the officers. As soon as the voting was over, I headed for Oklahoma to a doctor's appointment I don't want to be at.

I walk into the office and Kat is sitting there with Kim. I don't say a word to Kim, but I at least nod to Kat. Just as I'm sitting down, Callie walks in with Kellan and Devil in tow. I take the baby from Devil and hold him close. He looks more like his dad every time I see him "Devil you couldn't deny your son if you wanted to. He is you, made over." Devil smiles big.

"Don't I know it, but his temper is all his mom's." Yes, and he loves every minute of it. I need to talk to Devil for a minute, so I hand Kellan to Callie and kiss her forehead. I nod towards the door and Devil leads that way.

"I thought you were here for me. Not to talk to Kylar or see your daughter." Kim is being her usual catty self.

"Don't ever get my intentions wrong. I am here to see if it's a boy or a girl, but I'm not certain it's mine. The only woman I know is pregnant with my child is Em. I am not here to see you." It's meant to hurt her, but I didn't expect her comeback.

"Well, you're not running after her either, even if you are sure it's your child. She's gone back to where she came from and you're not there." *What did she say? Em moved? No.* I had things to take care of. I haven't even checked on her. Wait. How does Kim know where she is if she's not keeping tabs on her, and how does she know I haven't been there? I don't like this. Kat looks at her daughter and I know she realizes the same thing I do. I see Callie out of the side of my eye and now Callie knows, too.

"Kim, I don't know what you've been up to, but I can tell you this, if you go near Em, I will finish you. Are we clear?" I'm worried about Em now. I nod for Callie to go outside.

Once we're all outside, I make sure no one can hear us. "I was going to tell you Devil, but I realized Callie picked up on what was going on in there. Kim is still hooking up with Duke here in Oklahoma, and right over the Texas border. Kim is keeping tabs on Em. I didn't even know she was gone. I'll have to find out where she is and send Shield and Tazer after her." I take my phone out and send ZMan a text to find out where Em is.

"Who is Em and why did Kim say she's pregnant, too? Dad don't you know to wrap it up?" Nothing like getting told to wear a condom by your daughter.

"Emily is Joy's younger sister, and she's pregnant with your sister or brother. She has taken off somewhere and it disturbs me Kim knew that, and I didn't. I was shitty to her when she told me she was pregnant, and I haven't talked to her since. I wanted to deal with Kim first. That baby I'm not sure about. I used a condom every damn time, but I was stupid enough to use some Kim had and she had poked holes in them to get pregnant on purpose. Also, she hates you and Kellan, so beware. She's so jealous of you she can't see straight. She also had something to do with the whole Deacon thing. Not enough of daddy's attention and she wanted him to save her. Also, Stone is trying to out Devil and Steel from the MC. Did I remember everything Devil?" I look at him and he's just taking it calmly that I told Callie. They're smiling at each other "You already told her."

"To be fair, I picked up on some things about Kim and Stone and told Kylar and he confessed all the secrets, except for the Em thing." Callie has always been good at sniffing things out. I should have known she would figure it out.

"I had to make sure Callie and Kellan were always protected, and that she didn't trust the wrong person. Your daughter has a good head on her shoulders and she deserves for there to be no secrets. I tell her everything I can, and I will always make sure her, and my son are protected. They are my world. I'm man enough to say I love your daughter and I know she needs some time, but she will be my wife again, and this time for the right reasons." I believe Devil. Then Callie does something I never expected so soon. She reaches over, kisses him on the cheek, and smiles at him. Yeah, these two will be married again. She deserves some happiness.

Out of nowhere Kim comes out of the door. "If you want to see your child, get in here." I need to keep my cool with this woman, this may be my child. I need to come to terms with this. As we're walking back, I check my phone to see if there are any messages from back home and nothing. They're probably all still partying, so I text Brain and Blake. If anyone is still sober it will be them. I look at my watch and it's getting close to four. Surely someone can get back to me. About that time my phone dings. Brain received my text and they're on it. I relax some.

We get in the room and it's the standard thing. They ask her a bunch of questions, check her blood pressure, then the nurse asks her to lie back. She pushes her shirt up under her tits and pushes the front of her shorts down and tucks them in. She measures around her stomach and leaves the room. As soon as the nurse is gone, Kim grabs my hand and I jerk it back. "I just wanted you to feel the baby kick. Very active today." I place my hand back on her baby bump. It is moving around. I move my hand when she tries to put her hand on top of mine. "You don't have to be that way. We could be a family, if you'd let us."

"Not happening Kim. You got pregnant by deceiving me. I only fucked you to get even with Steel and Devil and to get information. I've never wanted you for anything else." Well that surprised her. She doesn't like rejection. "I won't change my mind Kim, so hang it up."

"You keep it up and you'll never see your child." Her first and last threat to me. I stick a chair under the door and turn on her.

"Do not threaten me Kim. You don't know anything about the man I can be. Push me, and you will see exactly how ruthless I am. I still know about your little boyfriend. What would Daddy Dearest say about that, and how fast would you be out on your ass? Devil already knows. Tempt me darling, and pictures will end up everywhere." I move the chair back.

"You wouldn't. I mean, I don't care." I know she's worried. All this revolves around her not getting enough of Steel's attention and hating Callie because of her goodness. Hating any woman who gets more attention than she does. I know now she will keep pushing, she can't help it, so I need to squeeze her boyfriend and Stone. Without them she will fall back under Steel and what he wants until she finds a new sucker. The door swings open and the technician comes in with the sonogram machine. I must calm myself down. Soon the doctor is in the room too, and Callie and Kat come in with the nurse. It's a full room. The doctor rubs the device with gel and starts moving it over Kim's stomach. We hear the heartbeat first and even if it happens not to be my child, the sound of a baby's heart is a miracle. Everyone is in smiles. The doctor moves it some more and we begin to see the form of the baby where we can make it out. Yes, a boy.

"It's a boy." The doctor says, and everyone seems happy, but you can tell no one is exactly excited. "Any questions?" We all say no, and he turns to Kim and tells her he'll see her next month.

The technician hands Kim the DVD and hands me pictures. I hand one to Kat, one to Callie, one to Kim, and I keep the other. Kat stays and helps Kim, but Callie and I walk out and meet Devil with Kellan. "Dad, you want to stay the night at our house?" Callie asks me.

"That sounds great coming from you." We both look at Devil. "You called it our house." He has it bad. Almost sickening.

"No. I have to get home and find out where Em is. I need to get her home." It slips out, but I don't regret it.

"Really Dad? Home? Does this mean you care about her?" Callie knows, but she wants me to admit it.

"Baby Girl, I do care about her. I think I fell in love with her without trying. Without wanting to, and now I have a lot to make up for, but I will do my best to make up for it." I know I need to try.

"That's good, Dad. I look forward to meeting her." That would mean a lot to me.

"Callie, you need to call Sarah. Her and your brother parted ways on bad terms. Well, she thinks it's bad terms. He's trying to let her go for her own good, and she doesn't get it, but she needs her best friend. Tazer was really trying to do something good. Just talk to them. I'm sounding like some gossiping old hen. Things I do for you kids." Here I am meddling. No not my usual self today. "Later." I need to get home. I leave to get on my bike and get some distance from here.

CHAPTER TWENTY

HOLDING
OUT FOR
FOREVER
BLACKPATH MC BOOK THREE

Em...

I'm in some pain waiting on the doctor to finally come in and see me in the ER. I'm trying to be patient; I am doing a better job than Joy. She's trying to drag any doctor she can find in to see me. I've been here for forty-five minutes and still no doctor. I've had to pee in a cup. They've taken blood. Checked my blood pressure. Asked me a million questions. I'm freezing because they had me change into a thin gown and said they would bring me a warm blanket, but I've yet to see it. I want to cry. I'm scared. I just want to know my baby is going to be okay. I'm tired, but every time I get comfortable I feel like I need to pee again, and it burns.

I woke up at 2:45 this morning with what I thought was just another trip to the bathroom in the middle of the night. Nothing irregular about that. I wake up every night one to three times with the urge to go. As soon as my feet hit the floor, I know something is wrong, because I have a sharp pain in my middle back that moves around to my side, and then it seems to go to my pelvic area. I finally get into the bathroom to relieve myself, but when I wipe I notice a pink tint and then I get a burning sensation. I go back to bed and try to get situated and comfortable but I feel the urge to go once more, and the pain starts again. I'm not too worried, I thought well, I didn't finish. So, I go to get up and I'm hit by a stronger pain. This time it completely bends me over. I get back to the bathroom and repeat my prior trip but very little comes out, but this time when I wipe, it is definitely red. I'm bleeding. I guess it's spotting. I've never felt like this, but then a pain hits me, and I'm terrified I am miscarrying by now, and I scream for Joy.

Joy comes running with a bat in her hand, our form of self-protection, and she sees me sitting on the pot and she thinks I've lost it. "What are you doing?" She looks around in my small bathroom.

"I'm in pain and there's blood when I wipe. What if I'm losing the baby?" I don't know what's happening.

"Let's get you to the hospital." Joy tries to help me, but the pain is more than annoying.

Now here I am at 4 am and still waiting, still in pain and still spotting. Joy comes back over to me with not one, but two warm blankets in her hands. "By the time someone gave them to me, I wasn't taking any chances. I grabbed two." She puts them on me and I think I have died and gone to heaven they feel so good.

"Thank you. They feel great." Just as I'm feeling warm the strong urge to go strikes again. I am trying to get up, Joy helps me, and I make it, but when I sit down, nothing, just burning. I decide to sit there for a few minutes. I'm tired of the back and forth. Then I hear voices. Nothing I can make out. The doctor is finally here, but who I see when I open the door shocks me.

"Em, how are you, babe?" There is the star of all my dreams, Chief.

"What are you doing here and how did you know I was here?" I am still hurting in more ways than one. My heart still hurts from the last time I saw him. I look at Joy and she looks guilty.

"He texted me; he was in town right after we got here. I thought he had a right to know what was happening, so I told him where we were. Sorry Sis, but he does have a right to know, even if he was an ass the last time you tried to talk to him." I nod at her. She's right, but even if she wasn't, I don't feel like arguing right now.

"It's okay Joy, you're right, he does. I'm just surprised to see him and still in some pain." I look at Chief and he takes hold of my hand to help me back up on the bed. Joy is there to help me cover back up. "Chief, why are you here? I mean why did you come?" He has to be here for a reason.

"I came to apologize and take you and Joy home. There's complications, and we need to talk about our child." *Who is this man and what did he do with the very angry man I talked to when I broke the news about the baby?*

"Chief, I'm glad you at least acknowledge the baby is yours. That's progress." I'm not trying to be a bitch, but he wasn't very nice the last we spoke. I feel the urge again; I'm trying to ignore it, but then I feel a pain again, and I scrunch up on myself. Chief comes to my side and grabs my hand.

"Are you okay? What can I do? Is it the baby?" Chief sounds concerned, and that's a complete turnaround for him. Just as he finishes, the door is pushed wide open and a doctor pulling a sonogram machine comes in with a technician on the other end pushing.

"Well Ms. Cass, how would you like to hear your baby's heartbeat? I'm the attending on duty, Dr. Greene." I would love to hear the baby's heartbeat, but I would love even more if this pain would ease up.

"Can you tell us it's sex?" Chief ask Dr. Greene.

"Who are you?" Dr. Greene is looking at Chief like he doesn't belong in here and like he is dirt on the bottom of his shoes.

123

"This is my child's father and that's my sister." I am short with him, but I don't like people who judge others by how they look. Yes, Chief looks intimidating with his scruffy face and he's wearing his cut, and has all those muscles, but that gives no one the right to judge him.

"Is it okay for them to be in here for this? And to answer that question," he looks at my chart and looks at me while I nod my head, "could be. She's far enough along. Let's see if the baby will cooperate." A nurse comes in the door and comes over to me and takes the blankets off and raises my gown up. Are they forgetting I'm in pain? The technician is getting the machine ready. When the gel hits my stomach, it's cold. Seems like they could warm up this crap. The tech reaches over and turns a nob and we hear the heartbeat. It takes my breath away. It's so strong. I relax a little. The doctor presses a little harder and I feel like I really need to pee. "There he is. Yes, a little boy. Congratulations, a son it is. Everything here seems just fine. Do you want pictures?"

"Yes." Chief speaks up before I have a chance. The doctor says something to the tech I can't hear.

"Nurse Jean, can you check and see if her other tests are in?" She leaves the room but returns shortly.

"Ms. Cass, your baby is just fine. Looking at these test results you have a urinary tract infection. Painful, and can be serious, but we'll try to get you fixed up. How do you feel about injections? I think an antibiotic shot would get this jump started if you're not against it." He looks at me.

"As long as it's safe for the baby, it's good with me. The sooner this pain goes away, the better." I give him a small smile.

"You are having spasms, and I'll give you something for that and it should ease it some. Drink lots of water. Completely safe for the baby. I will give you a script, too. Take it all even if you feel better before they're gone. Any questions?" I look at Chief and Joy. Nothing, but then Chief speaks up.

"Is this dangerous for our son or Em?" Chief sounds concerned.

"Mr. Black," The doctor looks directly at him. "Anything can be dangerous with blood loss, but spotting can also be normal. We watch kidney function closely during pregnancy, but a urinary tract infection is not a kidney infection, and if treated properly, is easily corrected, in most people. That's the reason I made sure she understands to complete all her antibiotics. She also needs to follow up with an office visit with her normal doctor. Plenty of non-caffeine liquids, preferably water, and rest. A good night's sleep will help to replenish her body. If she does these things and barring any complications, they should both be fine. The injections will help kick start the process." The doctor looks at me then to be sure I am paying close attention to her instructions and then back to Chief. "Anything else?" I shake my head no. The doctor and the tech leave.

"I will be right back with the doctors written orders and your injections." The nurse eyes Chief before she leaves. If she brings the shots to help me feel better, she could grab his butt and I wouldn't care. I wait until the door is shut and I think the nurse is out of hearing distance.

"Chief, what do you want? You can't stand to talk to me, and now you're here for what?" I see he's trying to be calm with me, but he doesn't like explaining himself. That's okay, I don't like him just showing up.

"Em, I don't like repeating myself. It's been a long day, but I will say this again. I apologize for the way I treated you. I know this is my son. I don't like excuses, but I had to deal with Kim that day and she tries the little patience I have. I found out she poked holes in the condoms, so I would get her pregnant. I'm sorry I took it out on you." *Why would she do that? It still doesn't excuse him treating me like that though.*

"What a bitch," Joy puts in her two cents worth.

"My thoughts exactly. I'm not even sure her son is mine. I mean, would you trust someone who did that?" He does have a point.

"I'm not leaving here. I just got my job back. I'm looking at houses to buy. This is home. We can figure out a custody agreement. I won't keep your son from you." I'm still in pain and I really don't feel like arguing right now.

"Em, it's too early in the morning to be arguing. I can bet you haven't had much rest. I've had none. I'm not taking no for an answer. After you rest today, tomorrow we're going down to the courthouse and getting a marriage license. We are getting married." I open my mouth to argue, but he puts his finger across my lips. "Don't argue. It will do no good. We are getting married. We are raising our son together, as a family. I have feelings for you, and I'm very attracted to you. I think you have some feelings for me, and I know you're attracted to me. I won't cheat on you, and you won't cheat on me. We will have a mutual respect and we will give our son a lot of love. I will do what is best for our son first before anything else." He thinks he can just tell me what I'm going to do. "Do you want to put our son through not having his mom and dad married? Do you want to be a single mom? Do you know how hard it is raising a well-balanced child with two parents, let alone by yourself? You can be a stay-at-home mom. It will be best for our son. Don't you want what's best for our son? That's what parents do. We'll discuss it later today, after we both rest. Joy don't you think we will be great parents together?" Chief looks at my sister and she looks like she's in shock.

"I think that's up to Em." Joy is quiet, which she never is.

"Joy, we want you back at the club. You did an excellent job and we all miss you." Chief is being too nice. It just doesn't seem natural.

"Okay Chief, what the hell is up with this kinder gentler you? This isn't funny, or your normal self. Spill." Leave it to Joy.

"I know I was very unfair to both of you. Especially Em. Dealing with Kim has made me appreciate Em. Not even that. Fuck, I don't know. I don't want to screw this up any more than I already have. I'm tired and rode a long way. I had to go to Oklahoma yesterday, went home and then we came here. Long day."

We need to table this until later. I'm hurting, and he's tired and as if on cue the nurse walks in.

"If you'll just roll to your side, we can get this done quick. Do you remember everything the doctor said?" I nod my head yes. I do not like shots, but if this pain will stop, anything is good. "Okay then." I roll, and she gives me two shots. Joy turns her head. She hates needles. "All done. I just need you to sign these discharge papers and did the lady out front get your insurance information?" I sign the papers and give them back.

"Yes, she got the information." In triplicate.

"Then you can go. Take it easy, Ms. Cass." She hasn't taken her eyes off Chief since she gave me the shots. Imagine that.

"Chief, if you'll step outside while I get dressed, so we can go. I want to go home and see if I can get some sleep." Chief has a little smile on his face.

"Babe, I've seen it all." He looks at my sister. "Will you go to the waiting room and ask Tazer and Shield to bring my SUV around?"

"You're not on your bike? You always ride your bike. Tazer and Shield are here?" Joy is happy, but she's tired too, so she sounds giggly.

"I couldn't very well come and help get you two home on my bike. I will explain about Tazer and Shield after we have some rest." So, there is more to this little visit. Right now, I'm too tired to care. I nod my head at Joy and she turns and leaves without a word.

I stand up and start to get dressed while Chief just watches. "Are you just going to stare? It's not like you haven't seen this all before." It doesn't take me long to dress. I just had on pajamas that are two sizes too big.

"I might have seen it all before, but I'm not going to turn down another chance and I haven't seen you with your stomach round with my son. That is sexy as hell." He has got to be kidding me. I didn't even brush my hair. My pain hasn't gone away, so I'm in no mood to flirt. I could sleep standing up.

"We're staying at some rental cabins. There are only two bedrooms, so you may want to find a motel, so you can sleep comfortably." At this hour, in this small town, they will be lucky to get anyone to open the door. In our small town, they lock the front door at midnight at the motel and it is after four in the morning and they won't reopen until eight. We don't get many travelers through here after midnight.

"What size beds do you two have and do you have a sofa?" Chief is crazy if he thinks he's going to sleep in my bed.

"Queen size, and yes we have a sofa pull out, but it's a small cabin." He needs to get the point that it's a small area.

"When I said we were getting married, it means you are mine and we will be sleeping together, so you might as well get used to it. Tazer and Shield have both fucked Joy, so I don't think she'll mind sharing a bed to just sleep, the pull-out sofa is a bonus. Now Em, I understand you're in pain tonight, but when I say married, I mean in every sense of the word. We will share our bed, our home, and our bodies. Come now, let's get you home

128

and get some rest like the doc said. When we get up, I'll get you some food and go pick up your meds." Chief is being a bossy ass, but like he said, it is late, or early. I just want my bed.

"You don't win. I'm just tired, so let's go." We will revisit this issue. He won't railroad me.

CHAPTER TWENTY-ONE

HOLDING
OUT FOR
FOREVER
BLACKPATH MC BOOK THREE

Chief...

After getting back to this little cabin at 6:30 am, getting situated, and finally getting some sleep, I feel better than I have in a long time. Holding Em while we slept felt right. My hand on her baby bulge put me right out. I felt my son kick for the first time. I forgot what that felt like. The amazement of it. I look at my phone and I have a few texts and two messages. I can get to those later. I should get up, but I don't want to disturb Em. She was finally able to get comfortable around seven and it wasn't long until she was out. I look at the time and it's after twelve. I slide myself away from Em and grab my bag and head for the shower. When Em said this cabin was small, she wasn't joking. Hopefully the walls are insulated enough the running water will not wake her up. I turn the water on full blast and step into the shower. I shocked Em this morning when I shucked all my clothes off and climbed into bed with her. Her face turned a bright red when my cock rubbed her ass. She was cute when she said I could have at least left my boxers on, but I left her speechless when I told her I wasn't wearing boxers. Commando I was. The hot shower woke me up and brushing my teeth made me feel human again.

I need to go out and get Em's prescriptions and get food for breakfast. Caffeine, first. Not much in this town, so I can't get lost. It's going to be a long day convincing Em and Joy to come back home, but I'm not taking no for an answer. The part where we're getting married may be a little more difficult, but it is what is happening. Today is Tuesday, so Friday we get married, and Monday we should be home. ZMan and Trigger should be able to handle everything until then.

Then my mind turns to Kim and how she's going to handle the news. She's a wildcard at best, and with Duke looming around somewhere, I need to handle this carefully with two babies factored into it. I never think of Kim's child as mine, but I better wrap my head around it, because there is that possibility. If so, I will have to find a way to co-exist with her for the next eighteen years. I never thought I would be a father again, and now I will have one more son, or maybe two. I'm going to have to come to terms with that, and soon.

After that, I will come to terms with being a husband again. It's like I told Em, I do have feelings for her. I am extremely attracted to her. She won't leave my thoughts and she is the woman I want in my bed. That is more feelings than I have had for any other woman in twenty years. I respect the hell out of her, and if anything ever happened to her there would be hell to pay. Just seeing her in pain last night was terrifying. I never felt so helpless, except for when it came to my children. I am at peace when I'm with her. I try to filter myself for her and I never do that for anyone. I have strong feelings for her and with that we can build something. She just needs to cooperate, and she will, because she's going to be a great mom and it's what's best for our son. I think until the DNA with Kim is confirmed one way or another, I will have to try to have patience with her, but everyone will know Em is my woman. I am going to claim her in front of the BlackPath MC as soon as I let Callie know there are changes on the horizon. Em has my son in her belly, by Friday she'll have my ring on her finger, when we get home she will have my patch on her back, and after our son is born she will be wearing my ink. I should have second thoughts about this, but I don't. I am at complete peace with it. Now to convince Em. When she let me fuck her without a condom she was as good as mine.

I look at Em one more time and try to quietly leave the room. I walk into the small kitchen and Tazer, Joy, and Shield are all up drinking coffee, and it smells great. I go to the cabinets and find a cup and pour me some morning wake up. As I do, I find myself whistling a little tune. I haven't done that in ages. The first drink of coffee is good going down. I pull a chair out and sit down and everyone's eyes are on me. "What?"

"You're whistling," Tazer sounds amused.

"You're smiling." Shield is on the verge of laughing.

"Damn Chief, you did not fuck my sister with her in pain. You are too damn happy for no more sleep than we got." I don't know if Joy is pissed, or shocked.

"Don't be crazy Joy. Em is still sleeping, and all we did was sleep. How sorry do you think I am? I thought we were friends." Joy must be sleep deprived.

"You're happy. Damn." Tazer is getting annoying.

"Em's bed is just really comfortable and I feel rested. After dealing with Kim yesterday, I needed it and it feels good." Anything away from that crazy woman is a plus.

"You're in love with Em and you won't even admit it to yourself. Damn, I like it Dad. It looks good on you." Tazer has no idea what he's talking about.

"I am giving you three a heads-up. As soon as Em is awake I'm telling her we are going to get a marriage license this afternoon and Friday we are getting married. I am claiming her as mine. I am putting a ring on her and I am moving her and Joy back home. No arguments and no excuses." I look at Joy and she's smiling real big. "Joy you still have your job and your room. If you don't want to stay at the club, you can stay with us, or I'll buy you a house."

"Don't you think it would just be easier to ask her instead of trying to steamroll her? She's not a club girl. She likes to think her opinion matters and she has a choice. Not a smooth move starting out on the wrong foot. Talk to her. If she thinks it's what is best for her son, she'll do it. I know she has feelings for you. She hasn't even talked to another man. She may be quiet and not have much experience, but if you try to take her choice away, you will see her stubborn side, and believe me, she has one. She can also hold a grudge for a long time, so if you think you have apologized enough—not even close. If you convince her to take the chance, she will give it her all. I will gladly go home. Tazer told me about Laurie losing the baby and I think I would like to talk to her about becoming a surrogate for her and Driller." Joy has shocked me. Why would she consider having a baby for Laurie and Driller? I don't even think they have thought of something like that. Would they consider something like that?

"Joy, I appreciate your input, but Em will have to get used to me. We will come to a meeting of the minds. I don't negotiate when it's something I really want. That isn't me and I am too old to change. We will work it out, or she'll just do what I say." Joy laughs and not a good laugh.

"What's the plan for today?" Shield is always wanting to get started.

"We are going to go get some food and get Em's prescriptions filled. Any suggestions on food for her Joy? I also want you and

Tazer to keep your eyes open for any signs of Duke or anyone associated with Kim. She's the one that let me know Em had left town and knew she had come home. That's too much information for her to know to be innocent. She's keeping tabs on Em and I don't like that type of bad around my woman." I have Joy's attention now. She knows the kind of twisted Kim is.

"Last week I kept feeling like someone was watching us. It was eerie. I didn't see anyone; it was just a feeling. The kind that makes the hair on the back of your neck stand up. It all started when Em's car wouldn't start one morning. I bought a bat to keep in my room." I don't like that at all. Joy is not the type of woman to spook easily.

"What was wrong with her car? Was it taken to a shop? Has she driven it since then?" I wait for her to answer.

"She took my car; I was busy unpacking. After she did her errands we went and looked at some houses her realtor wanted her to see. The lady she works for had her son come look at it. When he got here though, it started right up. I thought it was strange, but he said it could have been a loose battery cable. We used my car the rest of the week. Em has it scheduled for a look over at one of the shops here on Monday. Like I said, strange; then I felt like we were being watched. Also, if you want Em to take your plan seriously, you better talk to Mrs. Langston, her boss. The lady is more like family to Em, and she won't want to leave her needing someone." Joy is right, that is strange, and a thought comes to me. *If I wanted to keep tabs on someone but not be too close to get caught, what would I do?* Tazer gets up and walks outside.

"Joy write Mrs. Langston's phone number down and where the office is. Shield check Em's car over for trackers. That's what I would do if I wanted to keep tabs on someone. In this small town if it went to a shop they wouldn't find it. They wouldn't think to look for it. Most places wouldn't find it." I need to get these two home and safe. Joy gets a pen and paper and writes down what I ask and hands it to me. Shield goes outside with Tazer to start inspecting the car.

"I wrote everything down, and Em likes grilled chicken." Now to get going.

"Keep the doors locked and stay in. Don't answer the door to anyone unless it's one of us. I just want to be safe." I have an uneasy feeling, and I don't like it. The faster we can get home the better. I walk to the door and I reach down and take my extra gun out of my ankle holster and hand it to Joy. "The safety is on. Do you know how to use it?"

"I have an accurate enough shot. I know all the safety precautions. I won't let anything happen to Em. You know, she's a pretty good shot herself. Michael taught us both. Em used to go hunting with him. She's better with a shotgun or rifle, but he taught us how to use a handgun, too." That's good to know. As I open the door, I relock it and nod at her.

I get out by my SUV and Shield is looking under it. Tazer is looking over their bikes. Why are they checking our rides out? I'm worried about Em and Joy's. Shield reaches under my vehicle and I see he comes out with something in his hand. A very small tracker. It may be the smallest one I have ever seen. "Chief there was a tracker on each of their cars and one on yours. They weren't even hidden very well, but they are small. Em's car also seems to have a brake fluid leak. Those crazy women don't even lock their cars out here. I was going to check and see how much brake fluid is gone next. There's a big spot under her car, but it looks like someone has tried to cover it up, so it wouldn't be seen. I noticed because I was looking for a tracker, and it smells like brake fluid. I know we check your vehicles for trackers regularly at home, so this was either put on here, or right before you left home." Shield pops her hood and Tazer checks the fluid.

"It has none left at all. Our bikes were fine. Not us they want to keep track of. This has that bitch written all over it. You are going to have to do something to Kim to put her in her place. Em or Joy could have been seriously hurt in this car, and not only them but the baby, too." That is my thought exactly. I am not liking where my thoughts are going. Kim wants all my attention and she wants Em out of my life. I put nothing past her. If she'd stab her own blood in the back, then what is she capable of? Em and our son need protecting. I feel a huge urge to hide them safely away. Kim can't deliver that child soon enough for me. I take my phone out and text Joy to not drive anywhere, under any circumstances. I tell her about the cars being tampered with. I see her in the window and she waves.

"Shield stay here. Hide out somewhere and watch. Let no one in. We'll get everything we need in town and then when I get back Em and I will get that marriage license. I'm going to get them to tow both cars and have them checked out. Stay alert. Tazer we can both ride in the SUV." I can't afford to miss anything. I also need to make my calls and return texts. "Tazer you drive." We need to get back here.

CHAPTER TWENTY-TWO

HOLDING OUT FOR *FOREVER*
BLACKPATH MC BOOK THREE

Em...

I wake up in my bed alone. I don't even remember anything after I went to sleep. Usually I wake up a few times during the night. Not after we got home. After the pain let up a little I went to sleep and slept like the dead. I have the sudden urge to pee again, so I carefully get up hoping that the pain doesn't hit me again. It's there, but manageable. I take care of my morning business in my bathroom and make my way into the kitchen. My mouth is too dry. Joy jumps when I come into the kitchen. I guess she wasn't expecting me so soon. I don't see Chief or the other two, so I guess he's gone to get my meds. That's what he said he was going to do.

"We need to talk. Chief has gone to get food and your meds. Someone is tracking us. Chief left his gun here in case we have problems. There were trackers on our vehicles and they think your brakes were tampered with. Remember last week when I told you I thought someone was watching us? I was right. Chief is going to have our cars towed and checked out. If you had driven your car, you and the baby could have been hurt, or worse. I have never been so glad I am a procrastinator in all my life. If I hadn't put off unpacking, one of us would have been in that car." Joy must be kidding.

"Who would want to track us? No one cares what we do. If something was wrong with my car, then it's probably because it's time to buy a new one. I know I will have to buy a bigger vehicle before the baby's born. I just hate spending that kind of money before I have to, and I want to do some shopping for the safest choice." No one would tamper with my car, and it's not like we live way out in the boonies. We have neighbors, surely, they would let me know if someone bothered my car.

"Wake up, Em. Kim hates you. She knows Chief feels something for you. She knows you're carrying his child. She wants him, and she doesn't like the competition. She's not like you. She's vengeful. Do not underestimate her, and never trust or turn your back on her. I know you like to find the good in all people, but she has no good, and she has a long reach, or friends who do. Do you still have Michael's guns? I think you and I need to start carrying them. We have open carry now, it's legal. We have to protect your child, just think of it that way." I had rather be cautious than be sorry. I go to my bedroom and to the back of my closet where I stuck the gun box under a ton of winter clothes. Okay, not a ton, just my heavy warm clothes. I push them off and put in the combination and there are the two handguns Michael loved so much. I put the magazines in them. They are heavy. Not really the right size for me, but I am accurate with them. I make sure the safety is on both, then I grab the two boxes of shells out of the safe and shut it. I leave the boxes on the floor, take the guns back to the kitchen and lay them on the table.

"I have extra ammo on the floor of my closet. Take the one you want. You're right, better safe than sorry." Joy looks relieved I'm taking it seriously.

"Something else you need to be ready for is Chief. He is determined to marry you this week. He wants us to go home and he wants you as his ol' lady. He already loves your baby. Are you going to give him a chance? He's not good at asking. He lives in a different world than you're used to. He's claimed you, and in his world that makes you his. Are you ready for that? If not, you better get ready, because it's happening." Joy must be kidding. I still have choices.

"I understand an ol' lady is like a wife in the BlackPath MC, but I still have a choice. If I don't want to marry Chief, I don't have to. I can be a single mom. Kim is in my life because of him. I didn't do anything to her. I don't hate her. I feel sorry for her, except for the part that she really hates me. I don't know how I feel about Chief. Why would I marry him?" *Surely Joy doesn't buy into this?* There are a lot of single moms these days.

"I'm giving it to you straight Em. I will back you no matter what you decide. I always have your back, but don't you at least owe it to your son to think about the possibility of marrying his dad? It would make it easier on you. Your son would have you both. Chief is good to his word. He would be devoted to you both. You both have an attraction, and I think you two together would be better than you two apart. Two parents living in one house working together. Don't you remember when we had Mom and Dad. Mom was always fussing over us and we had Dad wrapped around our little fingers, but they were firm with us. It was the best of times and I never felt safer. They always put us first. Just think about it. Don't you want the same for your son? Chief is a good father. Biker life may be different from what you're used to, but you will have a huge family. A family that will lay their lives down for you and your son." Joy has taken my hand in hers. I remember the family life we were brought up in. I just don't know. I am deep in thought when the back-door handle jiggles, then I hear Shield's voice.

"Let me in. We have company." I grab one of the guns and open the door. He rushes in and locks it and closes the shade. "Joy

139

lock the front door. Hurry. Get in the hall. Are the windows locked?" I grab the other gun off the table and run for my bedroom. I hear the motorcycles in the front yard. I rush to my closet and bring the shells back with me. Joy comes into the hall and we wait for more instructions from Shield. "Where did you get the guns?"

"They belonged to my husband. I've had them locked up. Who's out front?" He looks at Joy.

"Chief should be here any second. He was only a few minutes out. You two ladies stay put. I'm going to check the front windows. If Chief is here, I'm going out front and you two do not open the door and stay away from the windows." Shield completely ignores my question.

It seems like we are in the hall forever and I finally have to go pee. I move carefully into my bathroom staying away from any windows. I take care of business and look at the clock as I'm leaving my room. We've only been in the hall twenty minutes. I sit down and just as I am getting comfortable someone comes in the back door. Chief yells out it's him and we can come into the kitchen. We make our way in there and all three men are there with food bags. Yes, my stomach is registering empty and I need my medicine and vitamins. I take the two guns and put them on the table, and Chief and Tazer smile.

"This pregnant woman needs food now and then medicine and then an explanation. In that order, please." I go to the refrigerator and get a water out. "Anyone else need water, tea, or milk?" I look at them. Each say water. I grab four more and my arms are full. I go sit at the table and Chief hands me a food tray. Grilled chicken salad. My favorite. Now my stomach thinks I have forgotten it for days. My mouth is watering. Tazer hands me a fork and I eat until I can't eat any more. I get up and take my medicine, put the rest of my salad in the refrigerator and I wait. No one has said a word. I look at Chief and he's deep in thought.

"How do you want our relationship to go?" *What the hell does that mean? Chief is confusing.*

"I want you to be honest with me." I thought he would know that. He looks at Tazer and Shield and then to Joy.

"The riders were with a local motorcycle club. They are loyal to The Feral Steel MC. Kim's dad is President of the Feral Steel. Stone convinced this MC that Steel wanted you watched. They swear they didn't tamper with your car, but they were lying. I had to call Steel to tell them to back off and tell them Stone isn't in charge. They have backed off, but I don't trust them. I think they're in Stone's pocket. Kim wants you away from me. You can't stay here. You're coming home with me. We're going to get a marriage license today. I talked to your boss. She understands. She's going to call you. This is non-negotiable." I look at Chief and then at everyone else in the room.

"Okay," That's all I say.

"Okay? You're not going to argue?" Chief expects an argument.

"No. I'll go shower and we can go to the courthouse." I get up and walk out. Leaving them all with their mouths hanging open.

CHAPTER TWENTY-THREE

HOLDING
OUT FOR
FOREVER

BLACKPATH MC BOOK THREE

C hief...

Kesler Davis Black was born five weeks ago. Two weeks later the DNA proved he is my son. He looks just like Ty when he was a baby. He weighed in at 7 lbs. 1oz. and has a healthy set of lungs. Kim kept with the K thing in her family, and Davis is Steel's middle name. We changed his last name to Black as soon as the test came back. Kim wanted me to stay for two weeks after the baby was born and I did, along with a very pregnant Em. We stayed at Devil's house with Callie.

Callie wasn't happy about the news that Em and I were married at the courthouse without telling anyone. We both wanted simple and that is what we got. We haven't even celebrated yet. It will happen but we want to get settled first. Em loves Callie and Kellan. We kept Kellan last night at our house, he loves his Em.

Kim threw one hell of a hissy fit when I came back with Em and Joy. She just knew she was going to be the next Mrs. Black. It would never happen even if there was no Em. I will treat Kim with the respect of being my son's mom, but she gets nothing else. I am watching her carefully, and if she doesn't treat my son right, I will take him and raise him. I know a child needs his mom, but she will treat him with love.

Callie is committed to Devil now and she's happy. When she came to pick up Kellan today she went to visit Tommy. Tonight, she's going to tell Devil she loves him. I am proud of Callie. She has grown so much. Her and Devil have taken their time to let their relationship develop and Callie has blossomed. I can't say I will ever like Devil, but I respect him for letting Callie have the time to heal from losing Dra. In doing that he has earned her love and devotion, and it shows in how happy she is. They both love Kellan and put him first. They are great parents.

Tazer is in an uproar. Right after we got back from our trip, Sarah's wedding announcement made the newspaper. He's fucking everything in sight. He shaved his head and went on several drinking binges. He'll work it out, but that's his story.

Joy talked to Driller and Laurie about being a surrogate for them. At first Driller was dead set against it, but Laurie wore him down. Joy went through a battery of medical tests and she is healthy enough. They've talked to a lawyer and they're getting the paperwork ready.

Em and I are waiting on our son's arrival. Ten days and counting. I've never seen such a beautifully pregnant woman. I don't know how I lived without this woman. She keeps me sane. She has a calming effect on me. Sure, we butt heads, but she has such a kind heart she usually ends up apologizing when I'm the one being an ass. She's taken to being an ol' lady like a fish to water. She cares about every member of the BlackPath MC. She lends a helping hand to whoever needs it. She checks to make sure the single brothers are eating right even though she must order them takeout. She can't cook worth a damn, but she tries. She did finally master breakfast. She says our son is going to starve to death. She's determined though, so she's enrolled in cooking classes and watches every cooking show on cable. She'll master it sooner or later, and if she doesn't, we have every restaurant on speed dial.

We still haven't caught up with Duke. He has Diamondback on his ass now. A few weeks ago, there was an exchange between Stealth and Duke. Stealth ended up shot in the back. He survived with a bum shoulder, but Diamondback has unleashed Sarge on him. Stealth is nursing the shoulder and then he will join Sarge. Shield is wanting a piece of him, too. The club has okayed it if Shield encounters him. So, Duke is a hunted man.

It's only two months until Christmas. Callie will meet her sisters, Micah and Maddie. She will love it, but she will also get sad news the same day. Her brother, Braun, is dead. Diamondback and he didn't have a falling out as rumored. Braun had cancer. The reason he couldn't have children was he went through chemo as a child. It made him sterile. His cancer had been in remission for years, but it came back, so he stepped down from his club, Rebellions 4Blood. Then he went to fight it again. He fought it, but it finally overtook him. His grave will be another one I know Callie will visit.

I'm laying here watching Em sleep. I do this a lot. Early mornings, I feel our son moving around inside her. I can't wait for him to get here and have him and KD together. Yes, he has a nickname from me already. He's a happy child and I love him more than life. I will love mine and Em's baby just as much, just like I do Callie and Ty.

I need to get up and start my coffee. I'm an early riser, but I let Em get her rest. I have things to take care of, so I can be off to help Em. I am just getting out of bed when I hear my phone going off. I reach for it and head for the shower. As soon as I see it I freeze. Killman has been attacked. I let them know I will be there in thirty minutes. I jump in the shower and take a quick one. I finish up and kiss Em bye. I get to the kitchen and grab my bike keys and then everything just fades to black.

"Wake up asshole. Don't you want to see me wake up your ol' lady. Today she gets a real man. I've got you where you can't get away, and you will have a front-row seat. I've already had Kim, and now I will have sweet Emily." Duke has my hands zip-tied and has me tied to a kitchen chair. All I need to do is keep him talking. My vision is blurry, but I see the small red light in the corner. Em and I decided not to take all the cameras out of the house until after she had the baby. She was smart to want an extra set of eyes on everything. We just took the ones out of the bedrooms. The knot on the back of my head is throbbing. "I would have gladly traded places with Stone, he was going to get a taste of your daughter while Devil watched. She is one hot bitch, or should I say, was. Yes, he was going to take Devil and her out with Kim's help, and then Steel. In fact, they should be getting here soon. Kim wants to see me break your bitch, then we're going to cut that baby out. That was Kim's idea. Nothing makes a man feel more helpless than watching his woman be fucked by another man." Duke is slurring his words. He's high, and there's no telling what he's capable of. He has me gagged so I can't yell out to warn Em. I wish I had told her I loved her. I've been going to do it, but I've been waiting for her to say it first. Now it seems so stupid. I see the other man coming in the back door. I don't know this man. I wonder if there are more.

"Duke, we need to get this over with and get out of here. We didn't get that call from Kim and she should have already called. Stone isn't picking up. I planted the stuff outside to make it look like the Rebellions 4Blood MC did this. I keep watching the road but nothing. It's daylight—anyone could show up." I see Em's feet in the hall. She is out of their eyesight, but then she's gone. Good if they just keep disagreeing, she will have time to get out and be safe. They can kill me. Em and my son need to be safe. I just hope KD is safe. What these pricks don't know is Callie had Bourbon and Rye's men watching her. Even if they made a move, she had extra security and Devil knew that. I have to believe they're okay. I know Callie will protect Kellan and KD with her life. My priority is Em. If she didn't get out, I am going to spank her ass. She knows to protect herself and let me worry about me. I look at the clock, another five minutes and someone from the club should be here.

"I am going to savor putting this piece of shit in his place, Cuz. Then I am going to blow his shit away. It's his fault I lost my club. That little redheaded fucker was his club's weak link, and he was so easy to distract. All it took was a yelping dog. All the fuckers will be at the hospital with him. He was a tough little shit though. Tougher than I thought. He took a beatdown and kept coming back. It took a bullet to the gut for him to stay down." I was supposed to meet Shield and Tazer at the club to go to the hospital with them. Brain was there, too. "I'm going to get the little woman. It's time we get acquainted." *Please be gone. Woman you better be gone.* Duke is making his way down the hall, staggering the whole way. I hear a gun go off, at the same time the back door busts open. I push off the table with my foot, so the chair goes over and shots are fired. It's over before it starts. The man Duke called Cuz is dead, bleeding out on my kitchen floor. Tazer is standing over him and ZMan is trying to help me up. All I'm worried about is Em. Shield is walking down the hall with a phone to his ear and Trigger is coming down behind him carrying Em. She's holding her stomach like she's in pain. ZMan finally gets my gag out.

"Is she alright? Did she get shot?" Zman has my feet undone and is starting on my hands.

"No Brother, she's in labor," Trigger tells me.

"Are you okay, Cam? I was worried. I was coming in here to tell you my water broke. I heard the strange voices, so I was quiet. I was sneaking down the hall. I just knew they were going to hear me." Em is crying and I'm trying to get loose to get to her.

"It's okay, babe. Why didn't you go out the damn window? I've told you. Think of our son first. He is more important than both of us." She jerks back, and I want to get to her and comfort her.

"What do you mean go out the damn window? I was having labor pains every few minutes and fluids leaking out of me. This isn't my fault. These people are here because of you. I heard what he said; he was going to kill our son because of some damn shit between clubs. It had nothing to do with me. I'm not some damn super chick." Em is writhing in pain and I wish I could take it away, above that she's pissed at me. ZMan finally has me undone.

"Thank you, Brother. You got here just in time. Trigger give her to me. I'll carry her to the car, so we can get her to the hospital." I try to take her, and she pulls away.

"Will you carry me, Trigger?" I look at him and he shakes his head no to her.

"Sorry, Em. You're Chief's woman; I can't do that." Trigger hands her to me. As soon as she's in my arms she stiffens up.

"Isn't the ambulance on the way?" Then she balls up, and I almost lose her from her being unbalanced. Trigger steadies us.

"We can't call an ambulance. The cops will come with it. I'll take you in my SUV." I just want to calm down before I say something I can't take back.

"So, you're bitching at me for not going out the damn window, but I can't go in an ambulance for our son's safety. If something happened the EMT would be there." I know Em is in pain, but she just needs to get in my SUV, so we can get to the hospital.

"Woman, I have to protect the club first." Em jerks again, but this time I catch what I've said. She goes completely still, and I notice everyone is staring at me. "I didn't mean it that way."

"Actually Chief, I think you just spoke the truth for the first time since we met. Now will you put me down, or I will jump, and we will both fall." Em is calm. Too calm. I set her down on her feet and she makes her way to the table. Joy walks in the back door and I know she's heard at least part of what's been going on. "Joy will you take me to the hospital so Chief can take care of his club? I need to go and have my son." Joy takes Em's hand and they start for the door.

"I'm going, too." Em looks at me with so much hurt in her eyes I can almost feel it.

"Take care of your club and I'll take care of my son." She looks at the floor and Joy is moving her towards the door.

"I'll be right behind you. I need to make sure everything is taken care of here. It's your first baby, so it'll take a while." Joy gives me a go-to-hell look, but I really don't care what she thinks. I won't be ten minutes behind them.

"I'll be right behind you." Neither of them looks at me, but everyone else is.

"Chief, if you don't want to lose that woman you need to go. She deserves better than this," Driller calmly says, but I feel his anger trying to get out.

"She'll be fine until I get there. I need to find out about Callie, KD, and Kellan. Duke said Kim and Stone were going to go after them tonight." Driller is looking like he doesn't believe what I'm saying.

"Do you know what I would do if Laurie could be going through labor with a child of ours? I never thought I would say this, but you are a real bastard." Driller looks disappointed in me, but he doesn't know the responsibilities I have. I can't let the cops find two dead men in my house with my brother's bullets in them. I have done this job for the last decade or so and it's who I am. Em must understand that.

"Devil called a few minutes ago. He and Callie are on their way here. They are bringing KD and Kellan here. Kim and Stone are gone. Devil had to shoot Kim. She was trying to kidnap Kellan. Callie and Devil both had her in their sights and Devil shot her so Callie didn't have to. He winged her. Callie would have killed her. Steel put a beatdown on Stone. Stone hit Kat and Steel went crazy on him. Devil said Stone had the drop on Steel, but when he backhanded Kat, Steel went crazy on him. Steel is getting his club back in line, but Devil put Callie and the boys first and is making them come here. He wants Callie and Kellan to be safe, so he can go back and help Steel. They also wanted KD with his dad. Bourbon and Rye are helping the Feral Steel MC hunt them down. I never thought I would respect Devil, but I do." Trigger is saying this to try to get me to go to the hospital. He's right. I need to go, but I must do one thing first.

"You're both right." Driller and Trigger both look shocked. "I'm going, and I hope Em will forgive me. Driller take charge. Tazer let's ride. Time to see your brother born. Driller be sure and let Callie know where we are and put double security on this house. Who is with Killman?" They all look at me.

"He didn't make it. Hammer and Cutter are with his parents." Tazer was close to Killman. "Felix is with them too." Oh shit. Felix is going to be devastated. After our son is born I need to go and see them.

"Let's get to the hospital. Trigger, you or Driller get Devil to the side and tell him, so he can tell Callie. She is going to be devastated." They nod their heads and Tazer and I leave so we can get to the hospital to see my son born. The ride to the hospital

149

helped clear my head. *How could I have said those things to Em? I have a lot to make up for.*

As soon as we get to the maternity ward, I see Joy in the waiting room and we go over to her. "What the hell are you doing here now? Don't you have to take care of your club first? Em doesn't even rate on your loyalties." Joy walks up to me and before I know it she raises her hand, but I catch it before it comes down on my face.

"Woman, what the hell do you think you're trying to do? Do not ever try that shit again or you will pick your ass up off the ground." I see the pain in her eyes. "What the hell is wrong with you?"

"While you are taking care of your precious club, my sister and her son may die!" Joy breaks out in tears, and Tazer steps up and takes her in his arms. She almost falls, but he catches her.

"Where is my wife and what are you talking about?" Joy can't quit crying, then a nurse comes in.

"Are you Mr. Black?" She looks at me like I'm the scum of the earth. Right now, I feel like the scum of the earth.

"Yes, I am." I need to for Em to be okay.

"Dr. LaTortue is in with Mrs. Black now. Mrs. Black's blood pressure is dangerously elevated and when she was having contractions the baby's heart was under duress. He also was not turned correctly, and your wife was not progressing as she should have, so Dr. LaTortue is performing a c-section. Normally you would still be able to be in there, but because of the other factors, she isn't comfortable doing this. Someone will keep you updated on that phone." She points to a phone on the table. "It shouldn't be too long, and your son will be here. He will be brought to the nursery and checked out and then you will be able to hold him if everything is alright. Any questions?" She looks at Joy. That just pisses me off.

"How is my wife?" She looks from Joy to me.

"Mr. Black, do you want me to be blunt, or sugarcoat it?" What the hell is she talking about?

"Nurse..." I look at her name tag. "Nurse Fouse, what the hell is the attitude about? If you have something to say, spit it out."

"Alright Mr. Black. When Mrs. Black arrived she was not only having strong contractions that were very close together, but her water had broken, and she was very upset. She was crying, and we thought she couldn't handle the labor pains. Some first-time mothers are that way. More nervous, so they just can't handle it. But upon further questions and checking her, we found her blood pressure was very elevated. She was hysterical. When we had her change from her street clothes she had scrapes up and down her right leg. When we inquired what could have happened, she would say nothing. She also was not dilated correctly. As in none. C-sections are done daily, and I'm praying your wife will be fine, but her distress when she came in was much more. Since her husband was absent, it had to have factored into the stress level she was in. Stress, Mr. Black, does not mix well with labor and giving birth. You said to give it to you straight and I hope your stress level can handle it." The contempt the woman is feeling for me is coming through loud and clear, and to tell you the truth, I feel the same way about myself.

"Nurse Fouse, is that your professional opinion or should we get your supervisor?" Tazer is pissed. "I'll be sure to let Dr. LaTortue know exactly what your update entailed." He is glaring at the nurse.

"Dr. LaTortue will be out to talk to you as soon as she is finished up. Be sure to be around." With that Nurse Fouse leaves.

"Joy, what in the hell happened between our house to here? It has only been..." I look at my watch. What seemed like only a few minutes has been two-and-a-half hours. *Well, hell.* It was eleven am, so she had been at the hospital for two-and-a-half hours without me.

"I couldn't get her to calm down. She kept crying and saying you just jumped to the conclusion she wouldn't try to get out the window. I think she was in shock or something. I told you she wasn't used to this damn life. She's not used to people breaking in her house and trying to kill her husband and seeing a man killed in front of her. Her water broke and it's her first baby and her husband was yelling at her. Then you had me bring her to the hospital. It's like you abandoned her. I don't know, Chief. You always take care of things, but you as much as told her, the club comes before her and your son. She couldn't handle it." Joy looks at the floor. "I think when this is over and Em and the baby are okay, that you need to walk away from them. You aren't cut out to be married, and she isn't cut out for this life." Joy gets up and walks across the waiting room and starts texting on her phone. Maybe she's right.

"This isn't your fault Dad. This is Duke's fault. Don't let that self-righteous bitch get in your head. Em and the baby will be fine. She said this procedure is done all the time," Tazer tries to reassure me. I see Callie come through the door and I feel the rage of a father as I look at her bruised face. Trigger and Shield are right behind her. Where is Devil? Why isn't he protecting his ol' lady? Just as I think it, I feel a ton of guilt descend upon me. *I just wanted to kill Devil for not being with Callie, but I had sent someone else with my own ol' lady to the hospital. What kind of screwed up is that?*

"Dad, how is Em?" Then she sees Joy sitting across the room and looks back at me.

"We are waiting to see. They are doing a C-section. Baby's heart was under distress when she had labor pains. She wasn't dilating properly. Her blood pressure was way up, and her water had already broken." She takes my hand and then she kisses my cheek. Callie is more than a daughter to me. She has grown into one of my best friends, and she always knows what I need, and that kiss helped. It was just understanding. Now I sound like some pussy, but Callie never judges me, and I love her for that. "Who do I need to kill for marking your beautiful face?" She smiles. She sits back in her chair and lowers her voice.

"As you know, Kim and Stone hit us last night, but they weren't alone. Steel and Kylar have trouble in the Feral Steel MC, and Steel has problems with Kat. Kylar brought the boys and me here and turned around and went back. Buzz and Ax were with us. Uncle Bourbon and Rye are helping Steel. I don't know everything, but the club is split and the ones following Stone are on the run. Kim was trying to take Kellan and KD. She had Leads with her. Me and him fought, and I shot him. My gun was knocked away when she hit me with a pipe. We fought. She had a knife and was going to stab me, I knocked it out of her hand. I got to my gun and was going to shoot her, but Kylar came in and winged her. This was at our house. Stone was at Steel and Kat's house. I don't have all the details, but Stone got the upper hand and he would have killed Steel, but he wanted his ma to go with them and she said no. Stone made the mistake of hitting Kat, and when he did, Steel went apeshit crazy on him and beat the hell out of him. Steel thought it was just Kim, Stone, and Leads who split from the club. He and Kylar took Kim and Stone to the clubhouse and locked them up, but when they went back they were gone. Fugulist and Pick are gone, too. They don't know if that's as far as it goes or not. Kylar wanted to stay, but I told him no. You gave Kylar the heads up about Kim and Stone, but Tito found out about Leads. Tito had been keeping surveillance on them and he had protected all the accounts from Stone. So they are on the run, but all the assets they have are what they have personally. They just don't know who exactly to trust. They are trusting the officers and everyone else is considered questionable. They are gathering the wagons, but Kat is torn. She is worried about Kim and Stone. The boys are great. They slept through it. Kelsey, Chelsea, and Laurie have them at your clubhouse. Uncle Trent has everyone on lockdown." I know there's more, but she looks nervous. Callie doesn't get nervous. She is cooler under pressure than most men.

"Spill it, Baby Girl." She looks troubled now.

"I called Krill and asked if he could come and maybe help. He said he was tied up, so I called Diamondback. I know you don't like him, and it wasn't my place to call, but my son was involved and Kylar and you may be too proud, but when it comes to Kellan and KD's safety, I will do what I think is right. Kylar yelled and raised hell and it's your turn now. Give it to me; tell me it's club business and not mine and it will do no good. Kellan is my son and KD is my baby brother—I will do what I think is right to protect them and the more eyes and resources available the better. So go ahead and let it rip. I'm woman enough to take it." She has that same stubborn look on her face as she did when she was little.

"So Kylar tore you a new one over it?" She gives me a crack of a smile

"To be quite honest Dad, it was mostly stress from the situation. I understand. His position in the Feral Steel MC puts a lot of stress and responsibility on him in situations like this. He doesn't want the club to look weak and me asking other clubs for assistance could look that way, even if the other clubs are family. I get it, but that doesn't mean I will ignore my gut feeling to ask for help so he can focus on doing his job instead of babysitting me and the boys. This isn't my first rodeo. He'll calm down when everything gets back to some sort of normal. His job is to protect the club. Mine is to support him and protect my boys."

She glances at me and smiles bigger. "Of course, he did say when I was back home he was going to redden my ass. Can't say that was much of a deterrent." She did not just say that. I look at her and she breaks out laughing. Everyone around us has not been able to hear the conversation, so they're staring at her. Joy gives her a hard glare. Callie just broke a big stress block for me, and I feel clear-headed again for the first time since my feet hit the kitchen floor.

"Baby Girl do not say that shit to me again. I don't want to hear anything about Devil spanking your ass." Tazer, Trigger, and Shield, all three shake their heads. Callie gets up and kisses my cheek and then goes over and gives Joy a hug. At first Joy resists but no one can resist Callie for long. Before long Joy is sitting there talking away to my girl. It dawns on me that Callie is the perfect ol' lady. She has seen how the club works from a daughter's point of view, and she knows how it works. Now she's making her way as an ol' lady. Devil is one lucky bastard.

I have done one big disservice to Em. She knows nothing about being an ol' lady except what she has learned on her own. As soon as she gets home, I will change that. I need to apologize for my actions today. I'm not used to feeling vulnerable and I was very aware she could be hurt. Not an excuse. It's been a long time since I felt like that. I can't go back, so I will do better going forward. I see Trigger staring. I motion for him to sit beside me.

"Did Devil tell Callie about Killman before he left?" Trigger looks tired.

"Yes. We are going to Felix's parents' house when we leave here. Everyone is there, and Felix was asking for Callie. Callie said she was going with or without us. You know how stubborn she is. She's taking Felix back to the clubhouse with her. He's packing up some clothes." I need to make sure I see him today. Felix is not close to his parents, and he will need everyone he can get right now. I also need to speak to Killman's parents.

A nurse comes in and she looks at all of us. "I'm looking for the Black family."

I stand and walk to her; I feel Callie behind me. Tazer has gone over by Joy. "We have your son in the nursery now. Mr. Black if you will come with me. You can come and wash up and suit up. That's if you want to hold your son. He is a sweetie pie. He weighed in at nine pounds and six ounces and twenty and one-half inches long. He is a big boy. Only baby in the nursery so all the nurses are cooing over him. He may be a bit spoiled before he goes home." I feel a weight lifted. He's here and I finally get to hold him.

"Is he healthy? How's my wife?" I need to see Em, too.

"Your son is doing great now. He came out screaming. The pediatric nurse in the nursery will give you a more detailed update. Dr. LaTortue will let you know about your wife when she's done. So, if you want to see him come this way. The rest of you can look through the glass window." I get up to follow her and everyone follows us. We come to another door and the nurse rings the bell and another nurse comes out and asks again if I'm Mr. Black. She already knows the answer. She was here when Kellan was born, so she puts the bracelet on. I leave the rest of them behind the door. I go through where I need to scrub up and they give me a cap and paper gown to put over my clothes. When I'm done, she finally leads me to my son. He is amazing. All ten fingers and toes. He already has little chubby rolls. The nurse hands him to me carefully, and I carry him to the big glass window where Tazer and Callie wait for their little brother. Callie has tears running down her cheeks, and Tazer has a big smile. Trigger and Shield are standing back with Joy and I see she's crying, too. I guess Callie and Joy just remembered their phones, because they have them out snapping pictures. I bring his head to my lips and I kiss it gently. The nurse nudges me and shows me the rocker. I walk over with the baby and sit and begin to rock him. I think he's fallen asleep when I see the doctor has come in.

"Mr. Black, I need to consult with you about your wife. Do you think you could come outside for just a few minutes?" I can see it's serious. I hand the baby back to the nurse and follow the doctor outside. By the time we're there, Callie and Joy have made it, too. We all sit down. "I'm taking it that it's okay to discuss this in front of everyone." I nod my head. "Mr. Black your wife has had some complications. Her uterus is twisted. I don't know when or how this occurred. After your son was born, Mrs. Black started hemorrhaging, but we stopped it. Her blood pressure is still elevated. Right now, she is stable and in recovery. We are going to do what we can to bring her blood pressure down. We are going to observe very closely and hope everything corrects itself. She needs her rest and she needs to be stress-free during this time. Mr. Black, I don't usually butt into my patient's personal business, but when your wife came into the hospital she was in a very emotional and stressed state. She doesn't need to return to that state of mind. I hope to have your complete cooperation in this situation. I am sorry if you think I have overstepped. I heard nurse Fouse was very rude to you earlier, and that is not my intention. I am only concerned for Mrs. Black's health." Dr. LaTortue is not being rude and I understand what she's saying. She is not being catty or a busybody. She is doing her job and I appreciate it. I stand, take her hand and shake it.

"Dr. LaTortue, you're doing your job and I understand. You have my complete cooperation. Thank you for the update and thank you for having her best interests in mind. I will do everything I can to help. When can I see Em?" She shakes my hand.

"Give them about thirty minutes to get all her vitals and get her situated. Only one person with her at a time. Remember, stress-free. She's only going to get to see your son for a few minutes, so she's already going to be one unhappy woman when her epidural wears off. Hopefully she will sleep for a while." The doctor leaves and I turn and look at my son. He is getting footprinted, and he is not happy.

"She's going to be okay. I was so worried. They are both okay." Joy looks like she could pass out. She is leaning on Callie.

I know how she feels. I need to apologize, and I need to tell her she means the world to me and it paralyzed me with fear to think Duke would hurt her. I took my fears out on her and I regret it. I will make it up to her and tell her I love her. I also realized that when I was tied up and waiting for the club to get there. I can't lose her. She must forgive me.

CHAPTER TWENTY-FOUR

HOLDING OUT FOR *FOREVER*

BLACKPATH MC BOOK THREE

Kim...

Why I thought I should let my stupid-ass brother and Duke plan last night out is beyond me. As usual, their plans go to shit. Now we're on the run and my son is not with me, and for some reason that really pisses me off. When I came up with the whole pregnancy idea I never wanted children. Why would I? I had no motherly instincts at all. I have never loved any man I would want to give a child to, but it pisses me off that Callie has my son now. If Kylar hadn't interfered, she would have bled out all over the nursery floor. I couldn't believe Callie outpowered Leads. I would have cut that bitch's throat in a heartbeat, but Kylar had to go and shoot me. Once again picking an outsider over family. If that wasn't bad enough, when we stop to get the cash, Keifer was blocked. Now all the funds we have to work with is the insignificant amounts Keifer has been slipping out of accounts. We have enough for us, but we had to cut Duke and Cuz out. They are on their own. Keifer, Fugulist, Pick, and I must stay one step ahead of them. No problem there, they are dumb as rocks. They thought we would stay locked up in the clubhouse. We still have one more friend left there that they know nothing about, keeping us one step ahead.

I know Chief is probably dead by now, so I must find a way to double back and get Kesler. No way is that bitch Callie going to raise my son until we can take Kylar and Dad out. Keifer is convinced we can get Ma to join us. He says she was just shocked at the change being so fast. She needs time to adjust. She'll have it, but she better make the right decision. I could use her help in manipulating Callie. If we take Kesler and Kellan, then Dad and Kylar will fall. They are weak when it comes to children. I think Callie is the tougher opponent. She's like a cat with nine lives.

I wish I could have called Duke before we took off. I need to know Chief and his woman are both dead. With Chief gone, that makes Callie more vulnerable and me closer to getting Kesler. Tazer doesn't even factor into this equation. He's a pretty face with no brains. He doesn't care about anything but club pussy and cold beer.

This damn shoulder wound hurts. It's a good thing I still have my stash Duke and I were sharing. I don't want to have to hunt down a damn dealer. It'll last me longer if I don't share. Keifer and his brothers are on their own. Dad had the bullet taken out and had me stitched up while I was locked up, but I'm limited on drugs to keep me from getting an infection. I'll see a doctor as soon as we're far enough away.

This shitty dive of a motel we are at tonight is not going to cut it. I guess for one night it will do, but tomorrow we should be far enough away we can upgrade. Leads was the brains behind the Feral Steel MC, so they will never track us. Even if they find us, Dad would never let them hurt me. If we're cornered, I'll just turn on Keifer and swear to Dad that Keifer made me help him. Problem solved. I can still get everything out of life I want. I just have a brat in tow now, but if I have Kesler, I have power.

CHAPTER TWENTY-FIVE

HOLDING
OUT FOR
FOREVER
BLACKPATH MC BOOK THREE

C hief...

Everyone has gone home. They finally have Em in a regular room and she has been sleeping most of the time. She wakes up long enough to ask about the baby and goes back to sleep. I was worried until Joy said she isn't used to any kind of drugs, so everything that puts her out does it for hours. The only thing they can figure out is the epidural meds. They don't usually make you sleepy. Apparently, they affect her differently.

The nurse brought the baby in a little while ago for me to feed. Em is going to be disappointed she can't breastfeed right now because of the medicine she's on. I just settle in and start feeding him when she opens her eyes. She is shocked to see us, but a big smile spreads across her face. She tries to sit up, but I see the grimace on her face. "Lie still babe, I'll bring him to you." He isn't happy when I take his bottle out of his mouth. He cries a little, but I am up and to his mom before he gets too fussy. Our boy has some good lungs when he's hungry.

"Can I feed him? Why does he have a bottle? I was going to

breastfeed him." Em is trying to sit up, but just can't get there, so I lay our boy back in his little mobile bed and go to help her scoot up. I get her there slowly. I am scared I'm going to hurt her. "Are you okay now?" She nods her head but I see the pain in her eyes.

"You can't breastfeed because of the meds you're on, so they give him bottles. You've been out a longtime babe. Joy said medicine knocks you out heavy, and it did. You were out all yesterday, and it's now close to noon. I was worried." Em is watching our son. She wants him now. "We need to give our son a name babe. All I've called him is Son or Baby. He is a hand-some baby and chunky—over nine pounds." Em just keeps watching him. I finally get him back to her and she reaches for him, and I see the tears starting. "Are you in pain? Do I need to get the nurse?"

"He's so beautiful. I can't believe he's finally here." She unwraps the blanket and she's looking at his toes and fingers. "He's perfect." He really is. "What was your dad's name? I know you've told me, but my head is kind of fuzzy." I look at her and she does look kind of pale.

"My dad's name was Whiskey." I grin. I see the look on her face and that isn't happening. Believe me, this world could not handle a second Whiskey.

"Well, that's not happening." I knew that, but Em is cute saying it. "Has there ever been anyone that had their real name be their road name?" Strange question.

"Sure. My dad and his two brothers, Bourbon and Rye." She raises her eyebrow.

"Did your grandma drink much?" That makes me laugh.

"No, never touched the stuff, but my grandpa was a different story. She always said she named her sons after the taste on my grandpa's breath when he knocked her up." That got a laugh from her.

"I was thinking Gage as a first name. I mean, I know nothing about road names, but it sounds good. That way I could always call him by his real name that we give him." I like it and she put a lot of thought into it.

"I like it and it sounds tough. It's a keeper." Her face lights up and I see Gage has finished his bottle. I grab the burp rag and help her position Gage to burp. "What about the middle name?"

"Cameron like his dad. Gage Cameron Black. I like it. It sounds strong and manly." That does. I like it. I like it a lot too.

"I love it Em and thank you for giving him my name." Now two of my sons have my name and the other has a nickname I gave him. I never thought I would have three sons and a daughter. My heart is full of love. "I love you Em. I should have told you that before, but I was too stubborn. I was waiting for you to say it first. I thought I would look less of a man saying it first, but I don't care what it looks like. I LOVE YOU! Is that loud and clear enough?" I take Gage off his mom's shoulder and lean down and kiss her.

"I love you too, Cam. I'm sorry I kept you waiting. I guess I was afraid you would reject me." She kisses me back and reaches for Gage.

"I'm sorry for the other morning and what I said. I didn't mean it. I guess I was in shock. I'm not used to not being in control and it froze me up inside." She gives me an understanding look.

"I understand, Cam. When I saw you were tied up, I thought I was going to pass out. Only the thought of our son kept me moving. I tried to get out, but there wasn't enough room. I tried. I scraped my leg. I called Trigger instead. That's how they knew where I was. So are you leaving the BlackPath MC now? You know since we have Gage. We can't let anyone hurt him. It's too dangerous." Em doesn't know what those words do to me.

I can't believe what she's saying. I thought she knew the club is part of me. I am part of the club. "No, Em. We are stronger together. The brothers and myself. We are family. All of us, including you and Gage." She must understand.

"No, Cam. That can't happen. I need to protect our son and I won't allow him to be put in danger ever again. You have a choice to make—us or the club." Em is ripping my heart out. She can't do this.

"Em, you and Gage are mine and I make the decisions. You're my ol' lady, my wife, and my world. I love Gage and will protect him with everything I am. I would die before anyone harmed him. Just like the rest of my children. I will protect you both just like KD. He is here, as well." She needs to hear me. She must understand.

"No, Cam. The things that happened yesterday will never happen again because I won't allow it. You have a decision to make and make the right one. If it's the wrong one, then Gage and I will be gone."

No way am I letting her leave me. She will not give me ultimatums. I get up and push the nurses call button and in just a few minutes a nurse comes in the door. "My wife is supposed to be resting, could you take the baby back to the nursery? I'll be gone for a little bit. I need to come by and fill out the birth certificate. We named him Gage." I can't even look at Em. I reach over and kiss Gage goodbye. The nurse wheels him away. I get my phone out and send Joy a text to come to the hospital. I need to get away for a while. I look at Em and I see a scared woman; I can do nothing to comfort her. She must come to a decision on her own to stay. I need to give it to her straight. "I only live by a few rules in my life and they don't change. Love my family. Protect my club. Ride free and never look back. If you can do those things with me then we can make it. If not, then you're not worth it. I gave my heart to you today and you spit on it. I can bend and compromise, but I will not fucking break my own rules. I love you, but I will not change me for you, so you have a decision to make and be sure to make the right one. If you make the wrong one, Gage and I will be gone." Then I turn and leave Em there crying. I turn to go to the nurse's station and I see Joy get off the elevator. I nod my head at her and keep walking. I fill out the paperwork for Gage's name and I leave so I can feel the power between my legs and the wind in my hair. Freedom of the road. I take off out of the parking lot and gun it to feel the powerful rumble. I need to escape just for a little while.

CHAPTER TWENTY-SIX

HOLDING
OUT FOR
FOREVER
BLACKPATH MC BOOK THREE

Joy...

I walk into Em's room and she is in tears again. What the hell did Chief do this time? I rush over to comfort Em and take her in my arms, but she moves back from me. "How do you live this life? The danger is too much. My husband picking a damn club over me and our son. I can't live like this. What do I do to get away from him?" Em just doesn't understand. No one has taken the time to explain it to her.

"Do you love Chief? I mean really love him?" I'm not giving her the reaction she thought I would.

"Yes, I love him. I have for a while now." Em is shocked by my words.

"Ol' lady lesson number one, if you love the man you stand beside him always. Not in front of and not behind, but beside. You accept nothing else." Em has stopped crying.

"Ol' lady lesson number two, you can give him shit in private if you don't mind the consequences, but never in front of the club or anyone else." I think I might have her attention.

"But I don't want him to be my boss, just my husband. I want him to protect my son from his dangerous life." My spoiled sister has reappeared.

"Ol' lady lesson number three, any brother worth his salt will protect every member of the club. That includes ol' ladies, and especially children. If you belong to a brother, then you belong to the club. The president is responsible for everyone. Cam is the president, so he has a lot of stress and as his ol' lady you can't add to it." She's listening. "That means every brother will put down their life for you and your son."

"So, if we're in trouble they will all come like the last time." My sister is dealing with stress or something. Information will help.

"Em, they will try to prevent it. This is not an everyday occurrence. This was done by idiots." She must understand it's not all danger.

"Ol' lady lesson number four, if you dis the club, then you dis the man. You can't give him ultimatums or try to make him choose. He'll walk every time." By the look on her face she did exactly that. "You'll lose every time."

"I messed up, big time. How can I fix it? I thought he would come back and fix everything. I just want to be safe and keep our son safe. I know dreadful things happen to good people. Michael dying proved that. I can't lose my son." That was the reason, she was thinking of Michael dying.

"Sis, you have to let Michael go. You can't compare the rest of your life to what happened to Michael. Terrible things happen and it's a tragedy, but you didn't die, and he wouldn't want you scared all the time." I've been trying to get her to understand this for three years.

"Can you find Cam for me? I need to apologize and hope he

accepts it. He told me he loves me, and I told him I love him." I knew they loved each other.

"Ol' lady lesson number five, he will come back when he's ready and don't force it. A biker on his bike is a biker at peace. Leave him to it, and if you're lucky, one day it will be with you behind him. Your hair blowing in the wind and your arms snug around his hard abs and your girlie parts getting up close to his body, the beast between your legs purring." I am almost poetic.

"Damn Joy, you make it sound almost sexual." Em has never been on the back of a motorcycle yet but it is time she experiences it.

"Only if you're lucky sister. Only if you're lucky." I wink at her. Thinking of...

"I need to change the subject for a second." I look at her and I have her attention. "I'm going to be pregnant soon. I signed the papers with Driller and Laurie. My treatments for the artificial insemination start tomorrow. Tomorrow I report to pin cushion duty. They start the injections, so I will produce more eggs. After that they will harvest and then fertilize. When they take, then they will implant." I feel good about it.

"Sounds like a science experiment, but I know Driller and Laurie will make great parents, and it's a very kind thing to do. Are you sure you can do it? You know, give the baby up." Em is concerned for us all.

"Em, the baby is not mine. It is Driller and Laurie's. I am their incubator for nine months. I have no desire to be a mom, now or ever. I'm not you. You are the nurturer. Not me. If I change my mind later, then I can still have another child. I promise, Em. Please just hold my hand." I need my sister.

"Okay Joy, I'll hold your hand. I'll do whatever you need." I am glad. I will need her.

"Killman's memorial is tomorrow. I'll be here with you while Chief attends." Em has a look on her face.

"Joy, I want you to help me. Is it at the clubhouse? I want to be there for Chief. I heard everything you said, and I should be there to stand beside Chief and help him. Can you get the doctor to let me out? Me and Gage. I want to surprise him. Please Joy?" She's right, and if it's safe I will help her. She will be Chief's ol' lady and be by his side. Right where she should be.

CHAPTER TWENTY-SEVEN

HOLDING
OUT FOR
FOREVER
BLACKPATH MC BOOK THREE

Sarge...

This stupid bitch I have in my sights thought she could kill Callie. I watch her, and she is as arrogant as her asshole brother. The man she was fucking shot my brother Stealth. Tazer shot Duke, and now I will take out the bitch who if left alive would be a thorn in that family's side until her son is eighteen. She's shooting that poison into her veins. It's no wonder she's crazy. No one else is with her in the hotel room. They have all gone out to party and left her here. Too bad. I could have killed them all at one time. She thinks since she's in a better place, she is safer. Not true. When I hunt someone, they are never safe. I hunt, I stalk, and I destroy. The Marines gave me the skillset; the club gave me a setting to hone my skill. These assholes gave me a place to execute it. Just a little further out of the shadows and I have my mark. One, two, breathe, squeeze, and she is no longer a problem for Callie. Kim is dead. Just like Karen. Callie is safe again and I am closer to repaying the damage I did to her heart. There is nothing left of my heart. I threw it away the night I fucked around on Callie. I will repay her until my dying day. That's all death is to me now. I feel nothing when I kill except redemption....

CHAPTER TWENTY-EIGHT

HOLDING
OUT FOR
FOREVER
BLACKPATH MC BOOK THREE

C hief...

Killman was honored today. He was a brave man who protected those he cared about. He was BlackPath to the bottom of his very soul. There wasn't a dry eye when Felix gave his love a touching eulogy. Michael "Killman" Martins was loved by all. When he came to us, he was soft and shy. He became skilled and someone everyone could depend on. Even after he earned his road name, Woody, his childhood nickname followed him. He will be missed. It was standing room only. The procession to the burial site was one that did justice for a member of The BlackPath MC. All the BlackPath MC, the Feral Steel MC, Rebellions 4Blood MC, and the BlackPath Warriors MC were present and led Killman to his eternal resting spot. We all said our goodbyes and honored him. Now we are headed back to the clubhouse to give him a send-off BlackPath style.

I haven't seen Em since I walked out of the hospital. I need to think, and she needs to think. My mind has been taking care of our last tribute to our brother. Em and Gage are always in my thoughts, but I needed space from Em. I visited Gage in the nursery last night, but it was late. Joy stayed with Em. I've spoken to Em on the phone, but there's a wall between us. She says she knows I have responsibilities and she's fine with Joy being there.

The thought of not having Em with me every day is not something I can embrace. I like having her with me, but I can't walk away from the club any more than I would be able to walk away from my children. It is in my soul. Sometimes I think it's in my DNA. I have told her my terms and what I need, she will either be there with me or I will learn to live without her. It will rip my heart out, but it is what it is. The wind and the freedom of this ride has built up the resolve I need. I see the clubhouse ahead and I will honor Killman the rest of tonight. Tomorrow tough decisions will be made.

We keep formation as we turn into the drive for the clubhouse. The prospect in the guardhouse watches as we all make it through the gates. He will lock us in when we are all inside. We are still on alert for trouble and we won't be letting our guard down anytime soon. When I park my bike, I see Joy's car parked up close to the front entrance. She should be at the hospital with Em. I wonder what she's doing here, then I can't believe my eyes. Em is coming out the front door with Joy behind her holding Gage. Em is not supposed to be home until tomorrow. Everyone is parked, and we make our way to the doors. I go to Em and she has a sad look on her face and there is doubt in her eyes. Callie, Felix, Devil, and Tazer make their way over, too. "Em what are you doing here? You're weren't supposed to get out until tomorrow." She looks at me and gives me a shy smile.

"Ol' lady lesson number one, if you love the man you stand beside him always." What the hell? I look at Em and then Joy. Joy is smiling.

"Heck yeah it is." Callie grabs Em's hand and pulls her in for a hug.

173

"I got that one right? I'm new and still learning, but I want to learn them all." She is still looking at me. My woman loves me.

"You'll never learn them all." Em moves her eyes to Callie to see if she's serious. "Didn't they tell you? The men add as they go. Something happens, and they make another rule. I've lost count." Everyone laughs at that. "Don't worry though, the consequences to not knowing a rule is usually as rewarding as learning them." Callie winks at Em. I am going to have to have another talk with Callie about sharing too much. I don't even want to know. I eye Devil and I'll be damned if he doesn't have a big grin on his face. I really should have killed him.

"I'm glad you're here, but are you okay? If you get tired you can go to our room." I don't want her to set back her recovery.

"I'll be fine with you and our family beside me. Let's go honor Killman now. He more than deserves it. I missed the funeral, but I want to be a part of tonight." I take my son from Joy and we make our way inside. I make my way to the front of the bar. All the food is set up and everyone makes their way in. I take Em to my normal table and I see they already have it set up for Gage with a portable crib to stay in and a couple others for the other two boys. They thought of it all. Callie makes her way back over with Kat beside her. Callie has Kellan and Kat has KD. My two uncles are there along with all our extended family. I put Gage down in his crib and go to shake hands with everyone and get everyone settled. Fifteen minutes later I see Felix has made it to our table and it's time to start. I make my way to the front of the overflowing room.

"I want to tell each of you that we are happy you all could make it to the BlackPath clubhouse this evening to join us. I am not a speech maker of any kind, so I'm doing this without notes. First, I would like to say at the funeral today we mourned the passing of a good man and strong brother, Michael 'Killman' Martins.

For what we lost and what should have been a much longer life. When we escorted his body to his final resting place we said our goodbyes to 'Woody and things that will never be.' This evening we are here for a totally different reason. We are here to celebrate his life and send off our brother's memory that will never be forgotten not only inside these walls, but inside each of our hearts. Share your stories and memories of him and drink a toast to a man that lived his life free and who always had his brother's backs to his dying breath. Everyone raise your glass." I reach behind me and get a beer and raise it. "Here's to Killman, salute." Everyone drinks and claps. I wait for it to die down a little. "Let's eat."

We made it through the day eating, drinking, and sharing stories of Killman. I see the day is taking its toll on Em. She has been by my side except for the occasional times I had needed a private talk with someone and then she would quietly excuse herself and help the other ol' ladies making sure everyone is fed and their glasses were full. She's never asked what our talks are about, or even raised an eyebrow when things were getting a little loud. Callie and Kat are taking KD and Kellan and putting them down for a nap. I make my way over to Em to help her with Gage. "Babe, do you need some help? I can go help you put him down." She smiles up to me.

"I've got it, Cam. I'm sure there is an ol' lady rule about not taking you away from gatherings where you might be needed." I see the tiredness in her eyes. She's trying to be funny, but I think she's too tired to care.

"I love you, Em." I know she's trying and I want her to know that so am I.

"I love you, too. I want to ride with you Cam. You said it was my choice and I don't want you to doubt for one minute what my choice is. I choose you. I will never ask you to choose between me, our sons, and your club. Your club is part of you and I know that, I was just scared. I'm not scared anymore." I love this woman. Then it dawns on me what she said.

"Our sons? As in more than one?" She nods her head.

"KD is ours, too. Right now, I'll need a little help, but he's mine, too. I want him to stay with us. He looks just like you Cam. We can go to court and get him." My world is complete now. I could never pick between my children. I knew Em had the capacity to love KD, but I was hoping she would want to help me raise him. Now KD will know the love of a good mom just like Gage. I will hunt Kim down and make her sign the papers myself if I must.

"Hold on tight, babe. This will be the ride of your life." I kiss the top of her head. I know the next eight weeks are going to seem the longest of my life. I finally have the woman of my dreams and it will be another eight weeks, while she heals, before I can fuck her. Damn my life. I bend down and kiss her again when I hear someone clear their throat behind me. I turn to look and there is Sarge and Diamondback. I look around and see ZMan and Tazer by the bar and motion for them to come over.

"Tazer make sure Em gets Gage back to our room and gets situated." He nods his head. He's still sulking because Sarah was here with a big diamond engagement ring on and wouldn't give him the time of day. Be careful what you wish for. Tazer wanted to let her go and he did, but he doesn't like the consequences.

"Gladly, and then I'm out for a little while, but I'll be back for the bonfire." Tazer has gone off the deep end. He came in a few days ago with his head completely shaved again. What's next? He gets Gage from Em and they head for the hall.

I motion for Diamondback and Sarge to sit down. ZMan has made it over and he sits, too. "Okay, what's up?" I look at Sarge and each time I see him now he looks further away. His eyes look dead. Diamondback keeps his voice low.

"Kim is no longer an issue. She's been neutralized. Callie doesn't have to look over her shoulder waiting for her to strike again. We have tabs on the others." Hearing Kim has been taken out brings me no happiness, but it does bring me relief. I know now KD can grow up in happiness surrounded by love and not have Kim's craziness touch him. I look at Sarge and I know he's the one who did it. That's why his eyes look dead. How many has it been now? When will he snap?

"Who do I owe?" I don't like owing anyone, but this time it's worth it.

"Let's just say it's payback for taking Duke out. He shot Stealth and the BlackPath MC took him out. Turn-about is fair play." Sarge's voice is flat and without emotion.

"Is that all it was?" I have to know.

"Chief, I won't lie to you. Anyone that ever tries hurting Callie, I will neutralize. She deserves better. She deserves everything. I broke her heart, and I will forever try to make up for it. She was my world and I destroyed it. Now all I can do is make up for it." I see he means every word, but how long until he breaks? He will do what he wants or what Diamondback tells him to.

"Diamondback, you helped us with the Stone situation, so I am giving you a heads-up—in December Callie will meet Micah and Maddie. We found out she has sisters and they will be here for Christmas. I am also going to tell her about her brother Braun. She has a right to know and it's time. You have until then to come clean with her, but I will not put it off a day past that. Do the right thing." With that I get up and head across the room to my daughter. I nod my head towards my office and she meets me there. We go in and I shut the door. She gives me a big hug.

"How's Felix? I haven't had much of a chance to talk to him tonight." She shakes her head.

"About as well as I was a little while ago. I can't believe this happened again to us. Killman was like a brother to me. I can't count the times he made me laugh or was just here for me. I'm going to miss him. Felix went home. He couldn't take anymore. Mr. and Mrs. Martins are with him. They treat Felix like a son; I'm glad he has that." Me, too. Felix's parents never have accepted he's gay. They faked it for a while, but their true colors showed through. Felix is a fine young man, and I consider him my son. I consider all of Callie's friends she grew up with as part of our family. They ate my food, slept in my house, and talked to me about their problems. The only thing I didn't do is carry them on my taxes.

"How are you, Baby Girl? You seem happier than I've seen you in a while. Are things okay with you and Devil?" Callie needs and deserves some happiness in her life. All the shit she's been through in her life is more than any one person should have to endure.

"Dad, I'm great. Really great. I haven't forgotten Dra, but I know he would want me happy. Kylar makes me happy. I don't know if I ever stopped loving Kylar when I started loving Dra. Does that make me an awful person?" I know this is something that is weighing on her, so I need to listen.

"No, it doesn't. It makes you confused and human." I know she has matured through all of this, but she is still my little girl.

"I was so hurt when Mase cheated on me. I mean, I just knew we were going to be with each other forever." I knew she still hurt from that. "With all my hang-ups from growing up with Karen as a mom, he knew how I felt about cheating. Then he betrayed me. It shook me to my core. Then here was Kylar and he was going to give me the means to put Tommy's murder to rest finally. I'd given up on the love thing, so why not an arranged marriage? But I fell hard for Kylar. Kylar made me wonder if what Mase and I had was even love or just attraction." Callie has been on a rollercoaster of emotion for a long time. "Then I found out Kylar betrayed me and I met Dra. Dra was a breath of fresh air. He swept me off my feet. He was honest with me to the point it hurt. He was my everything. I have never felt the pain I did when I was told he was dead. I thought I would go through life with no soul, but Kylar wouldn't let me. He has held me when I cried. Held me when I wake up from nightmares. He wouldn't allow me to crawl into a ball and give up. Him and Kellan kept me sane. I fell in love all over again and he wakes me up every morning with a kiss and a reason to smile. I will always have feelings for Dra. He holds a special place in my heart, but I love Kylar with everything I am. I need to tell you something, and please don't be mad." I look at her and wonder why she thinks I would be mad, but I see happiness and love in her eyes. I nod my head at her.

"You look so happy, Baby Girl. How could I be mad?" It's the truth. Anything that brings her that much happiness can't be bad.

"Kylar and I were married again yesterday. We went to the Justice of the Peace. I know we should have told everyone, but it's not the right time. We didn't want to wait though. Tomorrow is never promised and Killman dying proved that to us, so we just did it. It was just Kylar, me, and Kellan. Please be happy for me, Dad." I am. Devil has proven he can be trusted taking care of Callie and Kellan. I can't say I like Devil, but I do respect him and in our lives, that is more important. I get up and go to Callie and give her a big hug. My daughter has turned into an amazing woman.

"I'm happy for you Callie, but if that bastard ever hurts you again, I will put him to ground." Then I remember why I brought Callie in here.

"Sarge took Kim out. I needed you to know that, and I need you to be careful around him. He's changed. His eyes are dead Callie, and I think his soul is, too. Sooner or later he's going to snap, and I don't want you to be part of the fallout." I put her at arm's length, so I can see in her eyes she understands.

"I know he's changed, but I don't think he would ever do me any physical harm. No one would ever convince me of that. He's still Mase and he is still my friend. Could you get in touch with Krill for me? I am worried about him. When I called and told him about Killman, he seemed very distracted and he said he couldn't make it. Will you just check on him? I know I shouldn't be worried, but I am. He may tell you something he wouldn't tell me." I will have to keep a close eye on this because she is never going to take it seriously. It's better to just drop it.

"When are you and Devil announcing your marriage?" Give her something happy to think about and her mind off Krill. I don't want her running off to Colorado again. I will call him tomorrow.

"In a couple weeks when everything calms down. Now is not the time. Are you going to tell Devil about Kim? I like the way everything has been focused on me, so I wouldn't ask about you and Em. Is everything okay now? I know things were difficult for a few days." Callie is always good at sniffing things out.

"The waiting until you tell everyone is probably a better idea. I am going to brief everyone tomorrow about Kim. We all need an update. I know you need to tell Devil, but just ask him to keep it quiet until tomorrow. Em and I are going to be fine. We had a bump in the road, but it has been smoothed out. Now we need to get back to everyone." We get up and make our way back to the thinning crowd. I think I have just enough time to catch a little family togetherness before the bonfire. I sneak into our room and I see Gage snuggled in his crib. I make my way to our bed and toe off my boots and undress. I slide quietly in between the covers with my wife. She snuggles back into me and gets comfortable in my arms. This is peace. This is absolute. How did I get so lucky? Never ever is gone. Always and forever is my life now, and I will keep it.

EPILOGUE ONE

HOLDING
OUT FOR
FOREVER
BLACKPATH MC BOOK THREE

C hief...

We celebrated Killman's life last night with our honorary bonfire. We drank to his life and cremated his cut with honor. We told stories of how he had changed and grown with the BlackPath MC and how he will be missed.

Afterwards I went back to my room with my wife and two sons. After our nap in the afternoon we moved all of KD's things in with ours. With two babies, we will have to adjust, but I know my ol' lady is up for the task. As soon as Stone is taken care of, we will be back in our home with a lot more room.

Everyone was updated on the Kim situation. Steel and Sarge were nose-to-nose, and I know one day there will be bloodshed between the two of them. I don't know what Steel thought the outcome was going to be for Kim, but he took it hard—his daughter is dead. I would feel the same. Now he must tell Kat. They are headed back to their own clubhouse today.

Devil was here for the briefing, but once his dad was out of the clubhouse he disappeared with Callie. Kelsey has Kellan, so I don't even want to know.

Sarge and Stealth are on the hunt again for Stone and his crew. It won't be long until they find them. By the look on Sarge's face, he won't be around until the job is done.

I have one more thing to do before I go have lunch with Em. I can't put it off any longer. I don't like putting my nose in another man's business. I feel for Krill, because he lost his family all at one time, but he's a grown-ass man. I sit at my desk and make the call. It rings three times before he answers.

"Yeah." Krill sounds tired and pissed.

"Chief here. Callie wanted me to check on you. She's worried." I want this call done.

"Is she with you now?" Guess there is something he needs.

"No, she's been busy." Not going to explain that one.

"Are you sitting down? I have some news and it's going to shock you; you're not going to believe it." *Why the hell is he being so mysterious?*

"Krill, why are you beating around the fucking bush? Spit it out." I am getting irritated.

"Okay old man, Dra is alive." The line goes dead. *What the hell did he say? No.* I try to call back and no answer. I try again, nothing. I know I need to get to the bottom of this, so I go to the door and open it.

"Brain get your ass in here now!" *What the hell are we going to do now?*

EPILOGUE TWO

HOLDING
OUT FOR
FOREVER

BLACKPATH MC BOOK THREE

Callie...

I don't know what I did to deserve this man. I can't imagine my life without him. I think he owns my soul. He has us on the bed with not a stitch of clothes between us. He just wanted to hold and touch me. He has caressed and kissed every inch of my body, making me feel loved and cherished. I want more, but he isn't rushing. I run my hands up his back and feel every ripple of muscle and I want to feel more. He sits up and I see his hard cock between his legs, so I reach for him, but he slaps my hands away. He won't be rushed. He takes my foot in his hand and starts rubbing it, paying special attention to the insole. My back comes off the bed. He starts kissing slowly up the inside of my leg. God, I love when he does this. Then he kisses the other one. He slowly licks and kisses his way up to my belly, pulling my belly ring with his teeth. This man is a tease. He finally licks his way to my nipple and sucks it into his mouth and tickles it with his tongue while sucking it into a hard pebble. I feel him lining his cock up with my wet pussy and I try to pull it in, but he holds himself back.

"Babe, are you sure? We can wait. I don't want to rush you, but I want so bad to be able to be there for you every step of the way. To be able to hold you every night when you're carrying my child again. Are you sure?" He puts just the head of his cock slightly inside me. I try pushing so I can feel him completely inside me. The walls of my pussy are trying to draw him in, but he won't allow it until I tell him I'm sure.

"Please Kylar, I need you inside me. I want it. I want it so bad. I'm sure. God, yes, I'm sure. Give me your baby." He pushes his cock completely in with one thrust, and my back comes off the bed. It feels so fucking good. He goes in deep and grinds his hips and comes back out until all that is left in is the tip. Holy shit. Over and over, at a pace that is hammering the bed against the wall. I wrap my legs around his back and use my stomach muscles to pull him closer to me. I hear a growl come from him and it's like a fire igniting. I use my momentum to flip us over and I crush my pussy down on his dick. I need to come and I'm tired of being teased.

"Babe, you better get there, because I'm going to come." Kylar is moving with me now. We have sweat running off our bodies. He brings his hand between our bodies, finds my clit and starts rubbing our moisture around, and I am coming. My pussy starts contracting and I even feel it in my toes. Yes.

"God yes Kylar, I'm..." I can't finish. I can't move anymore, and I feel him flip me back over and he's chasing his own orgasm. He groans loudly, and I feel his cum shooting inside me.

"You're not leaving this room this weekend until my baby is inside you. Do you understand woman? You are mine and we are going to have that big family we want. I will never let you go again. I would kill anyone who tried to take you. You are my world. I love you." I know he loves me and I love him.

"I'm not going anywhere. I love you and I am yours and you are mine. Together forever. I love you Kylar Steel, and I want your baby in me." I am completely happy.

THE END, for now....

Making My Forever
Now Available
Tazer's story

NEVER
EVER

PART TWO

By Vera Quinn

COPYRIGHT

NEVER EVER

PART TWO

CHAPTER 1

NEVER
EVER|
PART THREE

C hief...

Another call-out for the third time tonight, or I should say this morning. I know we're hostile with the Dirty Rapture MC, but surely, we can have one night of more than a couple hours of sleep. At this rate we'll be too exhausted to put up a good fight. Driller and I received our calls to head back to the clubhouse. Grandma Sue is as much as raising Ty and Baby Girl, and Driller seldom gets a night alone with Laurie.

Whiskey wants all voting members there, now. No one argues with him; we just show up. He has been riding the edge of madness with his obsession of clearing out the Dirty Rapture MC. He says no one is safe with them trying to slip into our territory. I agree, but it's the way he has taken it upon himself to get rid of them that bothers me. They traffic women and children, drugs, illegal arms, and exotic animals. They annihilate anyone in their way, and we are in their way. Whiskey, Bourbon, and Rye, all three have put themselves in between the BlackPath MC and the Dirty Rapture MC. We fight as a family, but this time it's like they are on a solo crusade. They want to protect us all, but they need to understand that isn't what we're about. We always have each other's backs. We're stronger together.

As soon as I see the clubhouse, I know something big has gone down. Rye's bike is shot to shit and Bourbon's doesn't look much better. Whiskey's isn't even here. I thought he was calling from the clubhouse. Driller parks beside me and we walk in without even talking. The first person I see when I walk in is Trigger. He finally got off the fence and prospected with us, but he and Rye don't see eye-to-eye. Trigger is an undercover cop, and Rye doesn't trust the law.

Blake "Trigger" Trammel has been one of my best friends for years. The only other friend I ever trusted more is Tommy. We were inseparable for so long. Through thick and thin. Trigger helped me when we lost Tommy and helped me pull my head out of my ass when Cheryl cheated on me. No matter if he wears a badge or not, I trust him with my life. Right now, Rye is in his face. I need to diffuse the situation before Trigger goes off and does something that he can't come back from.

"Rye, what the hell are you doing?" He steps back from Trigger and looks at me.

"We were ambushed, and only you, Driller, Trigger, ZMan, and Ace knew about the drop. We are questioning everyone." It looked like it had escalated way past questioning. I don't like where this is going.

"Are you accusing Trigger of setting you up to be ambushed? That's what it sounds like Brother, and we all know he would never do that." I get between Trigger and Rye.

"Rye, I don't know what the hell has gotten into you, but I have never given this club a reason to distrust me. I am loyal to the bone. Just because I have a badge now doesn't mean I'm not loyal. Your problem is with the badge, not anything I have done." Trigger has always had our backs. I didn't agree with his decision to be a cop, but he's a damn man and didn't ask. No one in the BlackPath MC needs permission for anything. He has saved us from a couple of raids since he's been sworn in, and that is loyalty.

"You're damn right I have a problem with anyone that wears a damn badge. Not a damn one of them are honest." Rye has a right to distrust the law. His only son, Jace, was killed while in custody after a fight. He was found in his cell dead from a stab wound, and the security tapes conveniently showed nothing. Now Rye hates everyone with a badge, even Trigger.

"We have big troubles with a traitor in the club. Who would you suggest I blame? Everyone that knew has been here for a long time, and he is the only one to gain from it. I'm sure if there was a big split in the club, the law would love it." Rye is grasping at straws. "Who do you think we should suspect?"

"Maybe if Whiskey would finally legalize everything you wouldn't have to worry so much. You know change is coming and you just don't like it." Trigger is just as pissed as Rye and spewing hate that can't be taken back.

"Boy, you need to learn your place. You haven't been voted in for three months yet and you are preaching change. This club was built from us breaking our backs and spilling our blood. We have buried brothers and we are changing, but it will come at our pace, when we can make sure all the members are protected. We won't be crawling out on our bellies." Bourbon usually doesn't say much but seems Rye's bad disposition has rubbed off or he's just tired of being shot at. "We will find out who the traitor is, and they will be dealt with—club justice style."

"Where's Whiskey? He called for all members here. What does he have to say?" I want to find out exactly what has happened without brothers coming to blows.

"He was shot, we had to have Doc sew him up. He's in his room

changing. Don't worry, he has plenty of questions of his own."
Bourbon glares at Trigger, but he pulls Rye away and they go to
the bar to get a drink.

"What the hell is up their asses? I wouldn't betray the club. The
BlackPath MC and my brothers are second to only you, Ty, and
Baby Girl." I look at Trigger. I have always known club was a
second to the people he considered family.

"Trigger, you know they trust you, it's just hard for them to
understand why you want to be a cop. I know you would never
betray us." I hope he can understand why Rye would have reser-
vations.

"That's not what you were saying last week when I had Tina bent
over the pool table. You acted as if I had gone behind your back.
You said you didn't want anything else to do with her, but as
soon as I nailed her you went all territorial on her." Trigger is
right. I didn't want her, but I didn't like the idea of another
brother fucking her. I thought Tina was a good girl, but all she
wanted was the same as the rest of the bitches—a brother with a
cut to claim her.

"I told you that was a misunderstanding. It won't happen again. I
don't want another headache I can't get rid of. Cheryl taught me
my lesson in women." I don't think I'll ever trust another woman
again.

"Let's get this done. I want answers and I want them now."
Whiskey is as short tempered as Rye and Bourbon. We all head
down the hall to a meeting that will change things in a big way.
"Ace take everyone's phones and weapons." I don't know why
that bothers me today. It's standard procedure, but something
about the way Whiskey said it and looked at our SAA gives me
pause. "Give them to Rye to keep." Then he looks at Ace hard.
"Including yours." Ace's head pops up at the sharpness in
Whiskey's voice. Whiskey makes his way up to the head chair

and picks his gavel up pounding it loudly. "Everyone have a seat now. I want it damn quiet in here." Ace takes everything and gives it to Rye, then Whiskey nods at Bourbon. Bourbon goes and shuts the door and stands there like a guard. "Everyone should know by now we were ambushed last night. It was a setup. I am convinced we have a traitor among us." Whiskey looks closely at us all, but his eyes linger on Trigger and Ace.

"We lost absolutely nothing last night. For the last few weeks we have been missing money and some of the drug deliveries have been coming up short. There is a reason we have a rule of no drug use in the BlackPath MC. Users will do anything to feed their addiction, including stealing drugs. Number one rule in dealing with drug smugglers is do not ever let a shipment come up short. They may lose a little money, but not product. They know how much they have to the ounce. We have rules we live by when we go to war. We do not touch families as in women and children. They don't have these rules. So, when someone has sticky fingers they are putting every single brother, ol' lady, and child in danger. Does everyone understand this?" He looks at us with disappointment and anger in his eyes. "You are also being a traitor to the brotherhood." No one says anything. We are waiting for him to lay it out to us. I don't like the feeling I'm getting in my gut. "Last night we lost nothing because there was no meet. Bourbon, Rye, and I were setting up a ruse to smoke out our traitor. We have narrowed it down to two brothers." Whiskey looks from Ace to Trigger. "Rye check the phones." Everyone is starting to get restless and talking among themselves. No one likes being accused and no one wants to think their brother could do this. I know Trigger wouldn't do this. Even if he was unhappy with the club, he would never put Ty, Callie, and Grandma Sue in danger. Trigger doesn't even like our transports and Whiskey has left him out of them. In return, he doesn't get a cut of the money like everyone else. We only transport from one client to the next and Whiskey is working us out of the transport business. We are venturing into protection details. We may still put our butts on the line, but nothing illegal. We have families now and are being on the cautious side.

"This is the phone that made a call to an unknown number at the right time. It's Ace's phone. He had to of made the call when we were pulling out of the clubhouse. The times are almost exact. Trigger's phone didn't have a call going out until two hours later, and it was to Chief." Trigger did call last night, then he came by to see Callie and Ty before their bedtime.

"The only people that knew about the meet was Chief, Driller, Trigger, Ace, and Zman. The five knew specific details but after Chief, Driller, and Zman left, we purposely let slip our exact location of the drop and Trigger and Ace were the only two to hear. The only thing we had were bags of sugar, and they were all on my bike, which they took out, shooting me in the process. Another thing only Trigger and Ace knew, who had the supposed merchandise." Now we know why they're so pissed. No one could predict what happens next. No one would have imagined it would go this far.

Ace slumps down in his chair as if he's trying to disappear, but he comes up with a hidden gun from his ankle holster and shoots Whiskey before any of us can react. It all happens in a flash, but it seems like slow motion. ZMan is sitting next to Ace, before anyone moves he reaches over and disarms Ace, then snaps his neck. Smooth, clean, and he's dead. Not another gunshot.

Driller and Trigger are the first ones to Whiskey, with me right behind them. Rye has a gun out on everyone and Bourbon doesn't even move. Trigger is trying to do CPR and Driller has his shirt off trying to stop the bleeding, but there is blood everywhere. He has a gaping hole in his chest. I grab his hand and I'm telling him to hold on, but I know when his eyes close he won't be opening them again. I feel a loss beyond words. Whiskey was not a very loving dad, and he wasn't sentimental at all, but he was my dad and I respected and loved him. He taught me about life and how to survive and to hold the ones we love close. To protect our children and women and never look back. What's done is done. Just like that, he's gone.

I am so engrossed with what we are doing that I don't realize everyone else is standing back. Rye and Bourbon move over beside each other and have their heads together. It seems odd to me they aren't checking on their brother, but people deal with things differently, so I try not to over think it. I see ZMan is eyeing them though, so are Cutter and Trigger. This situation is tearing the BlackPath MC apart. I get up and approach Rye, get my phone, and dial 911. He doesn't stop me, but he doesn't like it. "What are you doing boy?" I've had enough of this situation. I knock the gun out of his hand and ZMan picks it up. I get in his face and let all my frustration flow onto him. "If this situation had been handled differently, this wouldn't have happened, but you three are always handling things without the rest of the club. Now you can see what happens when we don't work together. Whiskey is dead. I must tell Grandma Sue her son is dead. I must tell Callie and Ty their grandpa is dead. You three, with the help of Ace, have torn this club apart. Whoever sent Ace in here has achieved exactly what they meant to. No one trusts either of you. Hell, we don't even trust each other completely. How are we supposed to go forward from here as a club? Trust is the foundation of the BlackPath MC, and now there's none. We might as well disassemble and shut and lock the front doors. If you can't get your heads out of your asses and understand that, then you two are the ones that will hold us back. We are going legal. No more transportation of illegal arms or drugs. We'll put it to a vote. You can either help your brothers or get out of the way." I know I'm taking everything out on my uncles, but if they had just let this club work the way it is meant to, Whiskey might not be bleeding all over the floor. Just as I am thinking this, there are shots outside, and the window blasts open with a gas bomb. We scramble to get our guns, and the side of the wall is in flames. Trigger pulls Whiskey away from the window and Driller is trying to beat the fire out, but it's spreading. Slim has the fire extinguisher and puts it out. Rye gets the doors open, so we're crawling around on our bellies trying to get out. ZMan puts Whiskey over his shoulder and runs out of the room with bullets following from the window. I follow him and close the door. Everyone gets out. Driller has blood running down his arm and Hammer has been hit in the leg. If we had had more than two windows in that room, the outcome would have been a whole lot worse. I still have my phone, and I start calling Grandma Sue to tell her to lock it down until we can get there. Fortunately, Laurie was there with her to help. Grandma Sue has been in this life a long time and she is one tough cookie, so I know she can handle it until we get there. I pass the phone to Telly, so he can contact everyone else. He can send one of those group texts that I know nothing about, so more people can be warned.

Rye hands everyone their guns back and we are out the doors looking for the bastards that thought they could attack the BlackPath MC with no payback. There will be payback. There is no one anywhere, but there is a knife in the front door with a note telling us to get out because the Dirty Rapture MC is taking over our territory and this is our only warning. I feel a rage taking over my body. I know if it's the last thing I do that I will put every one of those bastards in the ground. Whiskey's death will be avenged and the BlackPath MC will not give up one inch of our territory.

"Rye call a lockdown. I want everyone here within the hour." I hear the ambulance in the background and I know we'll have this place swarming with people before long. "No, make that my place. Bourbon get the weapons and take them to my house. Don't ask questions, just do it now. We have no time to talk about it." Rye is on the phone and Bourbon has two of the prospects working with him. "Driller take the other two prospects and stock the house with all the food and supplies we'll need for two weeks. ZMan, get to your room and clean up. Trigger, when the law gets here can you deal with them?"

"Do you really trust me to do that? I mean the whole thing started with Whiskey, Bourbon, and Rye not trusting me." I look at Trigger and I know he has a point, but I never mistrusted Trigger.

"You're the only one I trust with it. I never doubted you for a second." Trigger looks like he accepts it as fact.

"When this is over, things must change, or I need to walk away. I don't trust Bourbon and Rye. They had their heads together right after Whiskey was shot and Rye took the weapons from Ace. He should have checked him for more weapons. In fact, he should have checked us both if they didn't trust us." *I just don't have the time for this right now.* "We'll vote after this is over, and my vote goes to you for President. Rye's going to want it, but he's not a leader, you are. He's the VP and should be taking charge right now, but he's useless in this kind of situation. Him and Bourbon both have always been followers, not leaders. You are a natural born leader just like Whiskey was. I'll take care of the cops this time, but after this, never again." I know now Trigger's days are numbered. The rest I just don't want to think about until all our loved ones are safe and Whiskey's death is avenged. "I'd almost bet Bourbon and Rye are connected to this and I aim to prove it. Whiskey was like a dad to me, and I will bring his killers to justice."

"Trigger, the only kind of justice I am looking for is club justice, and the law has nothing to do with that. Bourbon and Rye are family just like you, so we need to trust them right now. I trust them with my life, even above that, my family's lives. Just drop it before you say something you can't take back." The friction I thought was between Rye and Trigger has leaked over onto Bourbon. This will be dealt with after we have done what we need to.

CHAPTER 2

NEVER
EVER
PART THREE

C hief...

It takes the entire day to deal with getting Whiskey's body taken care of with Trigger dealing with the Sheriff's office, but it's finally done. Grandma Sue already knew Whiskey was gone. I saw the sadness in her eyes, but I never saw her shed a tear. Grandma Sue has lost a lot of people in her life, she just bottles it up and deals. When it comes time to say her goodbyes, she'll let it out. Right now, she knows she must keep it together for everyone else. Especially Ty and Callie. Whiskey and my children had a special bond. They got a side of him no one else did. I wouldn't call it a soft side, but an affectionate side. He loved spending time with them, teaching them things, and telling them stories. Ty and Callie were strong when I told them. Callie looked like she wanted to cry, but she watched her brother and he didn't, so she wouldn't let herself, either. Ty took her by the hand and read her a book until she fell asleep. My children are strong, and Whiskey helped make them that way.

The clubhouse is a crime scene, so we can't return there for a while. We have set up an office in my garage. Everyone has hunkered down in my house, that is everyone but Bourbon and

Rye. Good thing it's big. They have talked to Grandma Sue and they attend the meetings but come nighttime they leave. I know they have a cabin not far away they're staying in. It's where they have lived for the last twenty years when they weren't at the clubhouse. My house is too full for them, and they don't like being closed in at night. Whiskey was the same way. Telly has found some information about the Dirty Rapture MC, but for some reason I don't trust it. My gut is telling me it's a setup. I don't know if Telly is involved, or if it's just bad information, but for six months we haven't been able to get intel about them, and now suddenly, we can. No, too much of a coincidence. Telly has been our intel man for going on twenty years. He's been a good brother, so I'm hoping it's just bad information. I have a bad feeling he's involved.

I set up a meeting with Trigger, ZMan, Driller, and Hammer. I will inform Rye and Bourbon when they arrive in the morning. I want everyone to be aware of my feelings, but I want to keep it to the people I trust completely. As soon as the last one is in, I try to keep my voice as low as possible, so we're not overheard. "I don't trust Telly's intel. I'm not accusing him or anyone. It's just a gut feeling. It's too easy."

"Exactly what I was thinking. How do we suddenly get intel we've been trying to get for six months? I'm with you, gut feeling." Trigger lets everyone know his feelings right off.

"We have no other intel man. How do we check it out without accusing Telly? Bourbon and Rye aren't going to like it. They've been tight for a long time. They go way back," ZMan puts in.

"What about Hammer's nephew? He's young, but he's smart with anything that has to do with electronics. He built his own damn computer system. He took a bunch of old computers and made one that he can do anything on. He's way ahead of his time." Driller is right. The kid is only a teenager, but he is smart.

"That's a good idea. Who agrees?" They all nod their heads yes.

"Okay. It's a go. I'll stall Telly. Driller update Hammer and get the kid to work. Two guys go to him. Driller, you and Hammer would be good. See what you can find out. I wish we could get his phone, but that thing is so big it would be hard to sneak it. He hasn't updated to the smaller phone yet." Telly may be our intel man, but he's stuck in his ways. "I'll update Bourbon and Rye as soon as they get here, and I can get them alone." All the brothers look at each other. "What?"

"We know we have to deal with this first, but afterwards we want a vote. Bourbon and Rye haven't taken control like they should have when Whiskey was taken out. We think it's time for a change in the ranks. We want you as our new president. You have taken charge and we all trust you." Everyone is looking straight at me, except Trigger. He's looking at his feet, which is a sign he has something to say.

"I still think Bourbon and Rye are hiding something. I will get to the bottom of it if I have to start an investigation myself, officially." I knew this was coming.

"Trigger, can we just table this until our asses have finished this? I will tell you again that Bourbon and Rye would not betray Whiskey. Now just shelve it." I'm getting pissed at his insistence with no proof.

"Okay, Brother. Until this is over." We can get this taken care of, so we can bury my father.

"I'm with Chief. No way would either of my uncles turn on Dad." Driller is as hostile as I am towards Trigger's idea.

"The plan is set. Driller and Hammer go to Brian. Chief, you're bringing Bourbon and Rye up-to-date. We get this taken care of, so we can bury Whiskey in the style he deserves," ZMan sums it up.

CHAPTER 3

NEVER
EVER
PART THREE

C hief...

It's been three days. We found out Telly is a traitor, and Brian found out exactly how to take out the Dirty Rapture MC without even being there or risking our lives. It took a lot of convincing to get Bourbon and Rye to see that Telly was working with Ace to bring us down from the inside. After we convinced them, it took us all to keep them from killing him. We need him to keep feeding the Dirty Rapture information, so we can get everything set up. Tonight, is the night we end them all.

We convinced Brian to prospect for us. After the shock wore off that we wanted him in, he was all for it. Brian will take Telly's spot.

Tonight, we are to attack the Dirty Rapture MC compound. We know they're expecting us, so no family will be there. They think they're going to ambush us, so they will all be there. Telly told us it would only be prospects there tonight, so it would be an appropriate time to attack. It's all I can do not to rip his head off. As time ticks by, the need to see him suffer grows. I'm watching the clock. We have all our bikes ready to go. Bourbon, Rye, and ZMan are the only ones not here, but that's normal. They are the only ones that have left the last two days.

I watch the clock and just as the time closes in, all the brothers are in my garage. We have put all the women and children in the saferoom. Two prospects and Telly are supposed to stay behind to protect them. As it closes in on the hour, my phone rings. Driller and Trigger are on either side of Telly, so I answer and the voice on the other end comes in loud and clear. "Mission accomplished. No one came out alive." That was it. It's time to finish this.

"Telly, all of your friends are dead. All of them. That was ZMan, and their clubhouse that was supposed to be close to empty was full. Now it's blown to hell. No survivors." Telly looks nervous. He now notices Driller and Trigger are close enough to touch him. Trigger grabs his gun from his back and Driller does a quick pat down.

"I had no choice. I was deeply in debt to them and it was the only way I could repay the debt and stay alive." Telly is nervous and can barely talk.

"What was the debt for?" No one could owe that much money to betray your family.

"Gambling. It started on a few games a week and then I went to the ponies. I just got in deeper than I could get out." Telly is trying to make excuses for himself.

"We would have helped you if you had asked. Instead, you betrayed us and now blood has spilled because of your weakness. Driller tie him up and lock him in the shed. I'm going to tell Grandma Sue they can come out. Tomorrow we will all move back to the clubhouse. It was released today, and all the repairs will be temporarily fixed tomorrow. There's more room there.

Then we will give Whiskey his send off." I get up and move towards the garage door, but Trigger follows.

"I still think Rye and Bourbon had more to do with this." I have had enough of this.

"When we get to the clubhouse tomorrow, we will vote on every-thing. New officers, Bourbon and Rye, what to do with Telly, and if you stay or go." Trigger looks shocked, but I'm giving him what he asked for. I'm too tired to worry about it right now. Trigger is my oldest friend and I love him like a brother, but he must make up his own mind if he stays or goes. If he walks, he will no longer be my friend. No one turns their back on the club when we need them, and that is exactly how he's acting. Bourbon and Rye may be complete assholes, but they would never harm their brother. Trigger will have to accept that or walk away.

CHAPTER 4

NEVER
EVER
PART THREE

C hief...

It was a long, rough night. Bourbon, Rye, and ZMan returned to the house in the wee hours of the morning. They looked worn, like they had been in a war zone, and to be truthful I guess they had. Bourbon and Rye had spent the rest of the morning with Grandma Sue, which is unusual.

We returned to the clubhouse around ten and by twelve we are sitting in Whiskey's old office. It seems surreal he's gone. Day after tomorrow we lay him to rest. His body has finally been released from the autopsy.

All the brothers are sitting around. Rye stands behind the desk and whistles to get everyone's attention. Bourbon is to his right and Slim to his left. Trigger is standing over by himself. Everyone turns to Rye. "We're going to make this easy for everyone. Bourbon, Slim, and I want to branch out to Oklahoma and make the BlackPath Warriors MC. I know this will take a vote. I have some land up there and all I would be asking from the club here is backup if we need it. There are no other clubs there. It's in the mountains. We need a change and I think we all know this is what's best for the BlackPath MC." He takes a breath. "I'm asking for a vote, but we would like our votes to count for the officers." They are still members.

"I vote yes." Driller is the first to vote and we all follow behind with yes votes.

"Thank you. I think this is what's best for everyone. Any one of you is welcome to come with us, or just to visit," Bourbon puts in.

"I vote Chief for President. It's what Whiskey would expect. It's what was meant to be. He has shown in the last week he's a natural born leader and he will put the club first." Rye starts the vote and all votes are yes. I'm not sure I'm ready, but it's in my blood and in my soul. Rye moves over, and I take his place. Then I see Trigger moving forward and I hate what is about to happen, but there is nothing I can do to change it.

"I want to be voted out for now. I believe some of the members here had something to do with Whiskey's death and no one can change my mind. I will not accuse anyone now, but I will prove it and I will have them prosecuted. Whiskey was like a father to me and I can't just drop it." Trigger is walking on thin ice, but for some reason Rye is calm today.

"Son, I know you think we had something to do with it, but I guarantee we didn't. I'm glad you want to get to the bottom of it, but you will find nothing. I know this comes from a good place, but you're chasing ghosts that aren't there." Rye looks at Trigger like he feels sorry for him.

"Well, Rye. You're right, I do believe that. I'm not your son or anything else. If it takes to my dying day, I will be waiting for you to fuck up." Trigger just crossed a line he can't come back from.

"I vote for Trigger to be considered nomad, and he can't return unless he apologizes to the club." It's the only way I know of saving Blake from Rye's bullet. The vote carries forward. He removes his cut and walks out of the club and our lives. I lost Tommy to an early death and Blake to his badge. My two best friends are gone.

We continue to vote for new officers. Driller moves to VP. ZMan is voted SAA. Brian is prospecting, but as soon as he's finished he will be our intel man. Hammer is older but we all want him as our treasurer. He's fast with numbers and knows a worthwhile investment when he sees it. Hambone takes the road captain position and Cutter is the secretary. We have plenty of prospects, so our club will grow. We vote to rebuild the church room and build onto the clubhouse. We also vote to go completely legit. We have plenty of businesses to keep us prosperous.

The next vote is an easy one. What happens to Telly? Bourbon steps up and takes the floor. "Let us take care of him. Whiskey was our blood brother and we always had each other's backs. Rye and I should take care of him. The club wants to go legit, so let us take care of it." I agree they should. I would love to do it, but if I want to lead us into being legit, then this is how I need to lead.

Right after the vote was finished Bourbon, Rye, and Slim left the clubhouse for their cabin. In two days we will be putting Whiskey to rest and then they will leave for Oklahoma. The BlackPath MC has completely changed. We lost two traitors. Whiskey is gone and now I am president. A new chapter of the BlackPath MC. I feel loss. Loss of my dad. Loss of two men who helped raise me, Bourbon and Rye. Loss of my best friend, Blake. Trigger is gone forever and all that is left is Blake. My best friend who chose the badge over our friendship.........

The end, for now...

That is all for now. Next time the story becomes complete after Tazer's story. Never Ever will tell the story of Ty as a small boy who loses his mom, Cheryl. The story of Cheryl and Chief and how it affected Ty and his outlook on life. Hope to see you for the final chapters.

BlackPath MC

1. Never Forever

2. Catching Forever

3. Holding Out Forever

4. Making My Forever

Feral Steel MC

1. Beginning of the Inevitable

2. Beginning to Breathe, Again

3. Beginning of the Reckoning

Demented Revengers MC: Quitman Chapter

1. Surviving for Tomorrow

2. Surviving, One Day at a Time

3. Surviving Until the End

4. Surviving The Chaos of Life

Troubled Fathoms MC

Severed Ties That Bind

Stand Alone

Comfort Side of Heaven

CONTACT OR FOLLOW ME:

Email:

quinnbobbie.vq@gmail.com

Vera's Teasers:

https://www.facebook.com/groups/1083552724996044/

Vera's Reader Group:

https://www.facebook.com/groups/604946226544713

 facebook.com/veraquinnauthor

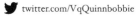 twitter.com/VqQuinnbobbie

instagram.com/quinnbobbie.vq

Made in the USA
Middletown, DE
22 March 2022